The Witnesses

The Witnesses

by Anne Holden

Harper & Row, Publishers

New York, Evanston, San Francisco, London

A JOAN KAHN–HARPER NOVEL OF SUSPENSE

STANDARD BOOK NUMBER: 06–011924–1

LIBRARY OF CONGRESS CATALOG CARD NUMBER: 71–156576

one

Sylvia reached out cautiously and picked up her watch from the table beside the bed. She puzzled over it for a minute. The small dial was hard to read in the darkened room but at last she made it out. Ten-fifteen; time to get dressed and go home. She had told the girls she would be in soon after eleven. She pushed back the covers and slid out of bed, carefully, so as not to wake Terence. It never took him long to pull on a pair of pants and a jersey; he could have a few minutes longer. She moved quietly about the room collecting her clothes, then let herself into the adjoining bathroom, closing the door noise-lessly before switching the light on. She blinked in the sud-den glare, then focused on the mirror above the basin and smiled at her reflection. She was pleased with what she saw. Even with her hair untidy and with no makeup left on, she was looking well—not beautiful, of course, not even perhaps especially young, but certainly not at all like a woman who had been married for nineteen years to Edgar Manson.

She lowered her eyelids, placed her hand on her hip, half turned in parody of an Edwardian chorus girl. "Sylvia Man-son, adventuress," she said aloud, and giggled. Terence made her feel like that, gay and frivolous and swinging. She had decided, months ago, that Terence was good for her.

She spun the dial of the shower and stepped under the jets of water, with a backward glance at the door. Sometimes when Terence heard the shower he came and joined her under it, but this night the door stayed shut. Probably sound asleep, and she knew what he'd say when she had to waken him. He would want her to stay, and when she refused, as she always did, he'd say, "But wouldn't it be great if you could stay? Don't you wish you could?" and she'd agree and say all the expected things, and mean them too, in a facile way, but deep down she didn't want any changes. Things suited her very well the way they were.

She sprayed skin perfume on her neck and breasts, dusted herself with talcum powder, put both flasks back in her handbag, and before dressing admired herself once more in the mirror. She was warm, glowing, suffused with animal contentment. At that point of time, that is at ten-thirty on the evening of Tuesday the sixteenth of January, Sylvia Manson was a happy woman. She was attractive, healthy, still under forty (by a few months); she had two pretty daughters whom she loved, she was fond of her serious, successful husband, proud of her home, enjoyed her way of life—all that added up to solid happiness, and then for the last year or so she had had Terence as well, to add sparkle to her comfort. Humming to herself, she zipped up her cornflower-blue dress—approved by both Terence and her daughters, unnoticed by Edgar—and leaning closer to the friendly mirror, she applied lipstick, eyeshadow, a flurry of powder. She gave a quick glance around to make sure she'd left nothing, not so much as a hairpin, then, satisfied, she opened the door to the bedroom, being careful to put the bathroom light out first.

Terence was still asleep. She hesitated by the bed, then on an impulse crossed to the window and drew the corner of the curtain back so that she could look out at the street. She liked the neighborhood where Terence lived, with its little shops and its foreign students, and its squares and rows of tall, narrow houses where people actually lived in attics and basements and one-room flats, all so different from her own tree-lined suburban street, where the solid houses stood foursquare behind their hedges and only the postman was seen on foot from one hour's end to the next. This view from Terence's window was like a stage set, especially at night when it was bathed in the orange glow of sodium lights. The ground sloped away from below the window where Sylvia was standing, then rose steeply again behind the encircling buildings, so that the various roads came into the little square at odd angles and were obliged to twist out of sight again soon after leaving it. There were flights of steps and darkened doorways, two or three shuttered shops, a telephone kiosk and curly cast-iron lampposts, perfectly placed for furtive assignations.

A cat ran diagonally across the square, and then, as Sylvia watched, a girl appeared round one of the corners, came onstage as it were, and began to walk along the footpath directly opposite. The night was so still that Sylvia could distinctly hear the tap of her heels on the pavement. She passed directly under a streetlamp and Sylvia saw her quite clearly, a young girl, with long, fair hair, wearing a short jacket and high, shiny boots. She had almost reached the end of one side of the square when Sylvia noticed the man. He came into view so suddenly that Sylvia thought he must have been there all along, standing in the shadow, perhaps staring up at the window while she had been gazing down into the street. Now, however, he was moving swiftly along the pavement, but his feet, unlike the girl's, made no sound. Sylvia, straining her eyes, saw that he was wearing white canvas shoes. Suddenly, she felt uneasy. Even at that distance there was something disturbing about the man, something stealthy in his swift, silent progress along the street. He didn't look like a man hurrying to catch a bus, or like an athlete out for a training run; he looked—the comparison came into Sylvia's mind—like a hunter, gliding along about a dozen yards behind the girl. She never once looked around but strode confidently on with her fair hair floating out behind her. She passed under another streetlamp and as she stepped out of the pool of light he slipped across it like a shadow, narrowing the distance between them dramatically until, as Sylvia watched, incredulous, he pounced.

The girl's scream sounded thinly through the glass. Feverishly Sylvia tugged the window up, then was absurdly embarrassed at the thought of shouting. "I say!" she made herself call, then called again, more loudly, "I say! You there!" but already there was the pounding of footsteps below in the street, the sudden blossoming of lights at the windows. Sylvia leaned out, trying to see the runners down below, and when she looked up again and across the square the man had vanished and only the girl was there, leaning against a wall, with her hands up to her face and her bag at her feet.

"What's up?" said Terence behind her. "What's going on? Who are you shouting at?"

Sylvia turned to face him. "Didn't you see anything?" she demanded, impatient at having to describe excitement instead of sharing it.

"Not a thing," he said. "I was asleep until you shouted."

"There was a girl," said Sylvia, turning to the window again. "You can see her over there if you look, and a man attacked her, sprang at her like a wild beast."

Terence stood beside her and peered out, shielding his nakedness with a shirt he snatched up. "She seems all right now," he said. "She's on her feet and there are people with her. Did your shouting scare him off?"

Sylvia considered. "I don't think so," she said. "I think it was the others coming up that made him run."

"It doesn't look as though they caught him, does it? They're all just standing around."

"He's had too big a start," said Sylvia. "I suppose someone's gone to ring the police, though. Oh, lord," she exclaimed on a different note, looking at her watch. "It's a quarter to eleven. I'll have to fly. Do hurry and get dressed, there's a dear. I don't fancy going out and getting a taxi on my own."

"Do you ever have to?" he asked.

"No, darling," she said, "but do hurry."

While he was dressing, she looked out the window again, but there was nothing to be seen. The girl and her rescuers had all moved away, and the square was deserted.

At breakfast the following morning Sylvia thought, as she often did, that the Mansons seen together around the table were like a family in a cartoon strip, or an advertisement. There was the mother presiding in her housecoat, and the two healthy, normal youngsters (perhaps, ideally, one of them should be a boy?) with their shining hair and their glasses of orange juice and their satchels of books. There were the checked curtains at the window and the striped china on the table, the gleaming refrigerator and the steam curling up from the coffee. And then there was Father, in his dark three-piece suit, hidden behind his paper, the hand emerging only to grasp the cup.

At a quarter past eight the girls left the house, at twenty-five past Edgar folded the paper, laid it neatly beside his plate and went upstairs. Five minutes later he came down again completely equipped for the city, and pecked Sylvia on her left cheek as she still sat at the table.

All this was routine, but this morning he said as he straightened up, "Weren't you home rather late last night?"

Sylvia was extremely startled. Edgar never showed the slightest interest in her activities, never asked her about her movements. This, once a grievance, had become a safeguard, and Edgar's question was a most unwelcome reminder of how much depended on his continued disinterest. Moreover, he had been quietly reading in his armchair when she had got in the previous night, and he had said nothing then about the time, which seemed to indicate that he had been thinking about it since, which was an uncomfortable thought. Now he was waiting for her to say something.

"Oh, I don't think so," she said, busying herself with the coffeepot. "Maybe a few minutes." With an effort, she remembered she was supposed to have been at a lecture on current affairs, one of a series run by the local women's club. "The discussion went on rather a long time," she said.

"Did you come home by bus?" he asked.

Now what? She hurriedly considered what to say. She normally let it be understood that she traveled by bus when she went out in the evenings, but there was always the possibility that someone had seen her get out of the taxi at the corner of their road. All the same, to say she had taken a taxi home would be to invite more questions. As a family, the Mansons did not take taxis. So she replied, "Yes, of course," with what she hoped was the right tone of faint surprise.

"I do wish you'd take the car," he said. "It'd save all that waiting around at bus stops in the cold."

She turned to face him and smiled in relief. He was only worried about her catching cold. "I never have to wait long," she said. "And you know how I hate driving at night, especially in the winter." In fact, she took a taxi to and from Terence's as a precaution. It was less risky than having to leave the car parked out in the street for anyone to see.

Apparently satisfied by her reply, Edgar was already moving toward the door. "Good-bye, dear," she called, in an excess of warmth, relieved the awkward moment was passed, moved by his consideration for her. He raised his furled umbrella in acknowledgment, then let himself out to walk the few hundred yards to the station.

Sylvia relaxed as the door closed, and poured herself another cup of coffee. Her turn with the paper. She quickly flipped over the pages, looking for sensation, then turned back to the front page to read the whole paper right through more carefully. Even so, she nearly missed seeing the account, which was tucked away well down on an inside page, but the heading "Another Girl Attacked" caught her eye just in time. She read it very quickly and realized it was not the incident she had seen, then read it again and was disagreeably struck by three points: the attack had taken place late the previous night, it had taken place in the district Terence lived in, and it was the latest one in a series of similar assaults on girls in that part of the city.

Sylvia pushed the paper away from her and went, tripping on the hem of her housecoat, to the bookcase in the front room. She took down a directory and looked up the street mentioned in the newspaper report. It was less than a quarter of a mile from Terence's flat. She thought of something else and hurried back to the paper. The first paragraph merely said "late last night," but farther down the column a man was quoted as saying he had heard the girl cry out at twenty past eleven. Thirty minutes and a few hundred yards were all that separated the attack she had witnessed from the one reported in the paper. The man had got away, and the girl, aged seventeen, was in a serious condition.

"Oh, God," said Sylvia aloud. She hovered irresolute for a minute, then went to the phone. Terence was pleased to hear from her, but she cut him short. "Have you seen the paper this morning?" she demanded.

"I read it at breakfast," he said. "As usual."

"And did you see the bit about that girl being attacked?"

"A girl? Do you mean the one you saw?"

"No!" she said, impatient. "Do go and get your paper. I want you to read it for yourself." She waited, tapping the mouthpiece nervously, until he came back on the line, then, "Look on page three," she said. "Third column, halfway down." She gave him a bare minute to read it before demanding his comments.

"Well, I don't know," he said, clearly at a loss to know what she was getting at. "It can't be the same girl, surely."

"No," she exclaimed, "but it's almost certainly the same *man.*"

"Oh, I don't think that follows at all," he said quickly, shying away from the melodramatic. "God only knows how many girls are attacked in the streets every night."

"In the same suburb?" said Sylvia.

Terence shifted his ground.

"They found this other girl straightaway, didn't they?" he

asked. "Well, they should be able to pick the chap up without too much trouble, and then we might hear if he was mixed up in the other business. That's if they bother to follow that up at all, which they probably won't. If you ask me, they'll get this man and we won't hear much more about any of it."

But Terence was wrong. In the evening papers the story had moved onto the front page. The girl had died, the man had not been found, and the press was having a field day.

Sylvia sat reading and rereading the reports, while her daughters did their lessons on the dining-room table and Edgar worked in his study. The girl who had died had been an au pair girl, "pretty," the papers said, returning from a students' club. She had been attacked from behind and flung, dying, into someone's front garden. The girl had cried out, the owner of the garden had come out and found her, in the meantime the attacker had run away. No one had seen him, no one had come forward with any information, the girl had died without speaking.

What gave the story its sensational news value, apart from the mindless savagery of the attack, was that there had been five known street attacks on women and girls in that same district in less than two years. This had been the sixth attack, and the worst. When, the papers wanted to know, would be the next?

Sylvia wondered if the five included the one she had witnessed the previous evening; she didn't think it could. The papers would have made a lot of an earlier attack on the same night as the fatal one, and none of them had mentioned it. Sylvia longed to ring Terence, but with the others at home and an extension in Edgar's study it was impossible. She

11

considered going out to call him from the phone box on the corner, but discovered she was afraid of the dark street, with its trees and hedges.

As soon as the others had left the house the following morning she rang Terence again.

"You haven't a shred of proof it's the same man," he told her. "The man you saw might easily have been a petty thief, out to snatch the girl's handbag."

"He didn't go for her bag," she argued. "He went for *her*. He pounced on her, like an animal."

"She wasn't hurt," he said.

"We don't know whether she was hurt or not. We don't know what happened in the end. Remember, it was late and we were in a hurry. You were getting dressed. For all we know, she was taken away in an ambulance."

"We would have heard the bell," he said.

"Then what did happen to her?" asked Sylvia. "She couldn't just have walked away."

"I expect someone took her inside," he said. "Gave her a cup of tea. Maybe someone drove her home. Certainly there was no one around when we came out, no sign of an ambulance, nothing at all."

"It was all over so quickly," said Sylvia. "Just like this other one. He pounced and ran away too." .

"Someone must have seen him running," said Terence. "With all this publicity they'll pick him up in no time."

But Terence was wrong again. Apparently no one had seen the man at all. Several days passed with no new facts coming to light, but the papers kept the story alive. People talked of Jack the Ripper and the police warned the women in the district to stay indoors after dark.

"It's beginning to look as though I must be the only person who saw this man," said Sylvia to Terence one evening in his flat. They were sitting up in bed smoking, reluctant to get dressed and go out in the cold. The weather for the whole of that winter had been exceptionally severe. Sylvia pulled the blankets closer around her. "It really worries me," she said.

"There's no reason why it should," he said, stubbing out his cigarette irritably. "It's not as though you saw the murder."

"No, but whatever you say, I saw the murderer," she said.

"That's nonsense, Sylvia," he said. "It's ridiculous to keep on saying that." She flushed; she was not used to criticism from him. "In any case," he went on in the same curt tone, "what *did* you see? The outline of a man in the dark, that's all."

"I saw more than that," she cried. "I saw him quite clearly. I tell you, I've got this mental picture of him slinking along on the other side of the square, and I remember all sorts of little things about him. Oh, I could identify him, if I ever saw him again, I'm sure."

He looked at her in amazement.

"I could!" she insisted. "Listen, I know how tall he is, for a start—about your height. And he was a young man. I could tell that from the way he moved."

"A young man, of average height," he said, with irony.

"And I know what he was wearing," she said stubbornly. "A black track suit, and gym shoes, white canvas shoes. That's why I thought he was an athlete at first. But the main thing I remember is that he had red hair."

There was a note of triumph in her voice. He was completely taken aback.

"But, Sylvia," he said, "you *can't* be sure of that. Red hair!"

"Why can't I?" she said. "He passed under two separate

streetlamps and I saw his hair quite distinctly. It was bright red, and it was brushed up in front like this." She showed him with a curl of her hand.

He stared at her. "But why didn't you tell me this before?" he asked.

"What do you mean?" she said. "I've been saying all along that I saw the man, haven't I?"

"But red hair!" he said helplessly.

"You know," she said, "if things had been different, I would consider it my duty to go to the police and tell them about this man. But of course in the circumstances I couldn't possibly."

"Because you were here, you mean?" he asked. "No, you couldn't really, could you?"

Sylvia should have been relieved that he had agreed so readily with what she had said, and in a way she was, but she felt rather let down too. She had expected an argument and she had marshaled a whole lot of sensible reasons for keeping silent that she wanted Terence to hear, so she settled back among the pillows and prepared to go over the matter with him.

But he moved away from her. "Time to get up," he said.

She was quite absurdly hurt by this remark, being mournfully sure that until then she had always been the one to say when it was time for her to leave. She found this reversal of roles ominous, she distrusted any change in their routine, yet a few minutes later, when they were out in the street waiting for a taxi, she could not resist saying, "Can we see each other tomorrow?" Hitherto she had always left it to him to plan their next meeting, confident that he would do so eagerly and soon, but tonight she felt a greater need of his company even than usual, and this was coupled with a sudden uncertainty about his next move. His earlier brusqueness, his readiness to show her out, trifling though they had been, had affected her like the first faint autumnal chill after a long hot summer.

Yet he replied promptly and eagerly. "Of course, dear," he said. "Terrific."

"But not in the flat," she said. "Please, Terence. Let's go somewhere else for a change. To tell you the truth, the flat's been getting on my nerves a bit lately. I'm sick of being cooped up here."

Terence was rather taken aback. Months before, the two of them had agreed that in their situation it was ridiculous to waste precious hours in restaurants or bars. Because it was far more pleasurable as well as much safer to spend all their time together in the secrecy of Terence's flat, they hadn't wanted to go out at all, but on this occasion they agreed to meet the following evening downtown.

Sylvia lay awake for a long time that night. The incident with Terence had left her nervous and disturbed; she resentfully blamed it on the unlucky business in January. If only she hadn't looked out of that window! She dozed fitfully, then jerked awake again with an uneasy sense that there was something wrong, something unpleasant but important that she should have done or would have to do. She lay tracing this feeling back to its source and soon realized that like Terence's abruptness it stemmed from the attack she had witnessed. In the silent darkness of the early morning she fancied she was being punished through Terence for her lack of action. It was suddenly not only obvious that she would

15

have to tell the authorities but also monstrous that she had not already done so. It stung her to think that if she had rung the police straightaway from the flat, the patrol cars would have been out searching the district and the other girl might not have been killed. Useless in this moment of truth to tell herself that the men who rescued the first girl would have reported the affair—they had not seen the attacker. She alone could have told the police what sort of man to look for, and she had kept silent.

Trapped in the still room, with Edgar sleeping quietly in the other bed, she felt a restless need for action to cancel out her earlier lack of it. She even considered creeping downstairs and calling the police right away, and she got as far as pushing back the covers, before pausing and trying to decide, for the hundredth time, what the consequences of telling the police would be. One fact dominated everything. She could not, could not, admit publicly that she had been in Terence's flat that evening. Edgar did not know Terence, did not know she knew him, there could be no plausible reason (except the real one) for her having been with him. Supposing she told the police on condition that they never revealed the source of their information? Surely she had read that the police sometimes cooperated with informers in that way? If what she saw had no connection with the later attack, all right, they might file her statement away discreetly, but what if her evidence was important? What if it was crucial, if they needed her to identify the murderer? She would surely have to do it openly, in court—no question then of being Mrs. X. And unless she was prepared to go through with it and actually give her evidence under oath, what was the use of approaching the police in the first place?

Shivering to think how near she had been to taking such a fatal step, she lay down again and tried to work out what else she could do. Supposing she made an anonymous call to the police, or perhaps to some newspaper, telling them to watch out for a redheaded young man in connection with the attacks on women? She began to work out the details. Calls could be traced. She would have to ring from a public phone box in some other suburb. She would have to disguise her voice, be careful not to let slip anything that could conceivably lead back to her. It was vague enough information, it would probably be ignored—by now hundreds of people would be coming forward with just such little snippets—it did not compare with an offer to identify a man who had been seen to attack a girl in that very area on that very night, but it would appease her conscience at no risk to herself. A little soothed at having come to some sort of conclusion, Sylvia slept again, and dreamed that she and Terence were chasing a red-haired man through a series of nightclubs, each one more grotesque than the one before. They finally cornered him on the grounds of Sylvia's old school. The hunted man turned on them and snatched off his red wig, and Sylvia saw that it was Edgar that the two of them had been pursuing all the time.

It was still very early when Sylvia woke again, but she was too shaken by this dream to go back to sleep. She found a cigarette and lit it, moving stealthily so as not to disturb Edgar, and tried to think of something pleasant enough to dispel the impression of haunting evil that the dream had left behind. Deliberately, almost fiercely, she concentrated on the dress that she was going to have made for Julie to wear to the end-of-term dance. They had chosen the material already—turquoise, to complement Julie's shining blond hair and bright blue eyes—and now she had to let the dressmaker know what style. Suddenly, without conscious transition, she was back thinking about the problem of communicating with the police.

In the cold light of morning, which was beginning to seep around the edges of the blinds, an anonymous phone call became ridiculous, impossible. Where would she ring from? Whom could she ask for? What would she say? She had always shrunk from making telephone calls, especially unpleasant ones, preferring whenever possible to write a letter, even sometimes traveling miles for an awkward face-to-face confrontation to avoid phoning. A telephone call was so impromptu, so easily misunderstood, so unsatisfactory altogether. After speaking even to Terence, she often found herself going over the conversation afterward, looking for nuances in his remarks, wondering if she had managed to convey exactly what she meant. How much more possibility of error existed in a furtive conversation with a stranger, a stranger moreover trained to be suspicious, if not hostile! No, she could not ring the police, but with her conscience aroused she would have no peace until she did something.

In the end, she fell back on her old solution; she would write a letter. That way, she could say what she really wanted to say. That way, if she was careful, she could avoid any risk of exposure. With a rather pleasurable feeling of excitement, of being involved in a drama without being overwhelmed by it, she began to work out the details.

The letter would have to be anonymous, of course—that went without saying—and an anonymous letter could not, or should not, be written by hand or on a machine that could be traced. In the end Sylvia decided to make her message up from words cut out of a newspaper. As soon as breakfast was over and the others had gone she would get a pile of old papers out of the closet and set to work.

After breakfast, though, she had second thoughts about the old papers, thinking that they could in themselves be a clue leading straight back to the Manson household. Instead, she put her coat on and went out to get a copy of a newspaper they never normally read, buying it not from the local news agent but from a seller up in the High Street, whom she had never seen before. She hurried home with the paper hidden in the bottom of her shopping basket, intent on putting the message together and posting it as soon as possible. Without even waiting to take her coat off, she sat down with the newspaper and her dressmaking scissors, then realized she would need a sheet of plain paper and some paste. She rummaged feverishly through cupboards and drawers, finally finding what she needed in Marion's room. It gave her a disagreeable feeling of guilt to be tiptoeing out of her daughter's room with the means of compiling an anonymous letter in her hands.

She soon abandoned the idea of cutting whole words out of the paper and began to snip each letter separately out of the headlines instead. It took her an unbelievably long time. At first she kept losing count and forgetting which letter she needed next, so she decided to stick each letter down as soon as she had cut it out. The letters were of all sizes, mainly large, and as she stuck them down one after the other they veered drunkenly across the page. The message was short enough, but she ended by using two sheets of paper to accommodate it. At the finish it read:

ABOUT THE MURDER OF MIREILLE SAMUEL THE AU PAIR GIRL, AND THE OTHER ATTACKS ON GIRLS. LOOK FOR A YOUNG MAN WITH RED HAIR, ABOUT FIVE FOOT TEN INCHES TALL, WITH A BLACK TRACK SUIT AND WHITE GYM SHOES.

It was very little, but Sylvia realized there was nothing more she could add, nothing she wanted to put in the way of a signature. She folded the sheets together, slipped them into one of the brown envelopes she kept for business correspondence, and using block capitals, addressed the message to the police station in the district where the au pair girl had been murdered. She then went out again and traveled two miles by bus before alighting to post the letter in a box on a street corner. It was Thursday, half day at the girls' school. She hurried home to be there before them. Once back, she realized she had not done the household shopping, nor had she started on any of the chores around the house. The letter had occupied her whole morning.

Sylvia went out a great deal, but she seldom went out two nights in succession. She would have said Edgar was not aware of this, but when she appeared in her coat that evening her husband, usually so incurious, chose to look up from his book. "Going out again?" he remarked mildly.

"Why shouldn't I?" she snapped in a tone that caused both her daughters to look at her. With an effort she controlled her nervous exasperation. "I won't be long," she said.

"Why do you have to go at all?" asked Julie.

"I just have to, that's all," she said. "I've got to see some people about the play the club's putting on in the spring." She was improvising, lying needlessly, something she was usually careful not to do.

Sure enough, Marion said, "You're not still involved with the play, are you? I thought you said that you've handed it over to Mrs. Ballance?"

Sylvia remembered that she had indeed said that, being afraid that the girls would hear through their friends' mothers that she no longer went to rehearsals. "There are a few ends to be tied up," she said. "After tonight they should be able to get along without me."

"Does that mean you'll be home more?" Marion persisted.

Dear heaven! What had got into the three of them tonight? "Maybe. I don't really know," she said, as vaguely as she dared, while making for the door. "I expect you'll all still be up when I come in." She sighed with relief as the door closed behind her, and almost ran along the street to the main road, where she would be able to pick up a taxi.

Terence was annoyed to find that owing to a reckless bus driver and an unusually cooperative series of traffic lights he had arrived ten minutes early outside the coffee lounge where he was to meet Sylvia. She would probably be a few minutes late, he reasoned gloomily, which meant a wait of a quarter of an hour or so, not long enough to venture far from the meeting place, too long to stand ankle deep in melting snow in a biting wind. So he sensibly went inside and sat down, choosing a table which gave him a clear view of the door and a segment of the street outside. He ordered coffee and prepared to watch for Sylvia in comfort, but he was soon distracted. This part of the city, which was strange territory to Sylvia, was familiar ground to Terence, who had once worked just around

21

the corner. This particular coffee bar was an old haunt of his and he had barely taken his first sip when two acquaintances came up, slapped him on the back and sat down for a chat.

So that when Sylvia came shivering into the coffee bar, having first waited outside for five minutes, she was indignant at seeing Terence in carefree conversation with two strange men instead of being as she had been imagining him, cold, solitary and anxious. He noticed her almost at once, settled her comfortably beside him, introduced her to his friends, ordered her coffee and cakes, but she was not appeased. She wanted to speak with Terence alone, and she was suspicious of these friends of his and vexed with Terence for telling them her name. He had not said "Mrs.," only Sylvia Manson, but she was conscious of her wedding ring, plain for all to see and very much at variance with Terence's possessive manner. She fingered her rings furtively under the table, wondering whether to slip them off, but it was too late for that. After all, she told herself, she could be divorced, separated, even widowed.

The conversation drooped and died, withered by her lack of response. The two men looked at their watches, shuffled their chairs back and went. Terence, who had been proud of Sylvia's handsome and elegant appearance on arrival, was embarrassed by her subsequent coldness.

"What's the matter with you this evening?" he demanded almost before the men were out of earshot.

Sylvia flared up, Terence retaliated. It was their bitterest quarrel yet. They patched it up and moved down the road to a pub, where Terence had two whiskies and Sylvia a brandy. Normally they drank beer and gin respectively, but each felt the need of an unusual stimulant that evening. They parted, apparently reconciled, but Terence had deliberately not mentioned a favorite record he had bought her as a present, and Sylvia out of pique had kept quiet about the letter she had sent to the police.

Sylvia got home at ten-thirty and went straight to bed, pleading a headache. She took time to gargle because of the brandy on her breath, then lay awake for a long time remembering how cheerful Terence had been when she had seen him with his friends. It seemed outrageous to her that the problems were all hers, that Terence was clearly not at all worried by anything. She was aggrieved; she began to think that Terence should somehow be able to help her. After all, she argued in the dark, in a way it was his fault that she was in this situation.

In the morning she was more rational, less inclined to blame him, but there was still an underlying resentment, a sense of grievance that she alone had been put in such an awkward position. Quite simply, it seemed unfair.

At dinner that night Julie said, "Barbara told me at school that she saw you last night."

Involuntarily, Sylvia glanced at the head of the table, but Edgar was over at the sideboard looking for the mustard. Had he heard? Had Julie deliberately picked that moment to speak, thinking her father would not be listening? "Saw me?" Sylvia repeated, but softly.

"Yes. She said that she and her mother saw you over in Gillies Street."

"What on earth was Barbara doing over there?" asked Sylvia peevishly.

"What's that got to do with it?" said Julie, opening her eyes wide. *What indeed?* "I think they were visiting an old aunt or something. Barbara says they saw you coming out of a restaurant."

Saw me, or saw Terence and me? "I was nowhere near Gillies Street last night," said Sylvia crisply. "They must be mixing me up with someone else."

"I told Barbara that," said Julie. "I said you were at the club."

"I wasn't actually at the club," said Sylvia, taking fright. "It's so cold there these nights that we decided to meet in someone's house instead."

"Whose house?" asked Marion idly. But was it entirely an idle question? Examining Marion's smooth fourteen-year-old face, Sylvia could not be sure.

"Mrs. Miller's," she said at random. She had read somewhere that Miller was one of the commonest surnames. "Does anyone want any more potato?" Under cover of the ensuing chatter she went over what had been said. She knew already that it had been a mistake to have been so definite. She should have said something like, "Oh, yes, I was over that way. We had to collect some props." Too late now, after such a flat denial. She could only hope that the girls would forget all about it or, failing that, that Julie would be able to convince Barbara that she had been mistaken. Sylvia also wondered whether Edgar had heard; she thought not. Over the years he had become oblivious of family conversations, and habitually ignored any remark not addressed directly to him.

Sylvia thought about this disturbing little exchange often during the next week or so, but as it was not referred to by anyone, she eventually almost forgot about it. Unknown to her, however, Julie had questioned Barbara again. Barbara had shrugged. "It *was* her, you know," she said indifferently.

"Mummy saw her too. We both knew it was your mother right away." Julie said nothing about this at home.

In spite of her feelings of pique, Sylvia had no intention of staying away from Terence. She longed for him more than ever and she hardly dared to leave the house in case the phone rang. It was three days though before he called—it had never been so long before.

"Why didn't you ring days ago?" she demanded before she could stop herself.

He sounded surprised. "I could hardly call you during the weekend," he said, "with all your family at home." He always avoided mentioning Edgar by name.

"You have before," she said, and thought with pain of those delicious elliptical conversations they had carried on, with her watching Edgar through the window as he pruned the roses and busied himself at other Saturday tasks.

All Sylvia's misgivings vanished, however, when Terence opened the door of the flat to her that evening. He was so familiar, so nice, so pleased to see her. They put a stack of records on and went to bed, and it was as good as it ever had been. Afterward, though, when she should have been relaxed, she was tense and fidgety.

"I wish *you* would ring the police," she said out of the blue. "It's your flat, after all."

"What about?" he asked, startled. "Oh, you mean about that business the other week. You're not still on about that, are you?"

"Of course I am!" she cried. "And so should you be. Why can't you just ring up and say what we saw? You needn't say anything about me, after all."

"Hey, wait a minute," he said. "*I* didn't see anything."

She was petulant. "You must have," she said. "Surely you did. I called you, didn't I?"

"Not really, and by the time I got to the window it was all over. Oh, I saw the girl with the people standing about her, but nothing else."

"You mean you didn't see the man at all?"

"Of course I didn't. You know I didn't. What are you getting at?"

"You would have seen him if you'd come over to the window as soon as I called out."

"I was asleep, wasn't I?" he said, indignant at being accused. "I could hardly come bounding over to the window in my sleep!"

Sylvia was silent for a moment, and when she spoke next it was in a different tone, softer, almost wheedling. "Terence," she said, "couldn't you say you saw that man? No, listen, all you'd have to do would be to repeat the description I gave you, red hair and so on. After all, you were right here. You could *easily* have seen him."

"But I didn't," he said.

"Wait," she said. "Look, I saw him, didn't I? But I can't ring the police and say I was here in this flat, can I? But there's nothing to stop you ringing on my behalf."

"No," he said.

"You mean you won't?" she cried. "What's the matter? Don't you believe me? Don't you think I saw that man?"

"Of course I believe you," he said, "but don't you see, I can't possibly ring the police and say I saw something I didn't."

Sylvia argued and pleaded, but he was adamant. She had been so confident of persuading him that she dressed in an angry, hurt silence. She had meant to tell him about the anonymous letter but faced with what she thought of as his lack of understanding she could not bring herself to mention it.

For the next few weeks nothing new happened as far as Sylvia and Terence were concerned. They met twice a week, as usual, but although they avoided mentioning what they cautiously referred to as "the January affair," they found they were bickering rather often over all sorts of trivial matters. Then in March, late one night, as it happened a night when they had met, another girl was attacked in a nearby street, and when they read about it in the morning papers it was immediately apparent to both Sylvia and Terence that the weeks since the previous attacks had been a hiatus, a time of waiting for something else to happen.

Sylvia wept when she saw the girl's photo. She was seventeen, like the other one, and she looked like Julie. Sylvia went to the telephone and got hold of Terence before he left for work.

"Do you see what's happened now?" she said in a low, furious voice. "Another girl might be dying, and you could have stopped it just by making a phone call."

"Wait a minute," he said, angry in his turn. "Don't you try and pin this on me! You're acting like a spoiled child, Sylvia, looking around for someone else to take the blame. I didn't see that blasted man—you did."

"But you know I can't call!" she cried. "You *agreed* I couldn't call! And how can you say I'm spoiled, when it's not myself I'm thinking of at all, it's all these poor girls? If I *was* spoiled and selfish I'd just forget all about it."

"Yes, I'm sorry," he said. "I shouldn't have said that, but

surely you can see I can't ring the police and tell them a pack of lies."

"It's not lies," she said stubbornly. "It's the truth. What does it matter which of us was actually looking out of the window?"

"We've gone over all this already," he said wearily, "and anyhow, what if I had rung? Do you think if I'd said, 'Watch out for a red-haired man!' that that would have made any difference? Don't make me laugh."

"It would have been a lead. It might have been all they needed to be sure who did it."

"Not bloody likely."

"If this girl dies," she demanded, "will you ring the police then?"

"I've got nothing to say to the police," he said. He put the phone down and hurried to the office, but once there he could not concentrate. He was in love with Sylvia. She meant more to him now than she had done months before, at the start of their affair. He still dreamed daily of marrying her, if it ever became possible, and these frequent arguments with her left him shaken and upset. Moreover, he was by no means as positive about the whole business as he had sounded when talking to Sylvia. Maybe the information she had was vital, who could tell? Perhaps the police were watching several suspects, unable to decide between them, and if one of them had red hair, what then? Would Sylvia's evidence be conclusive? But lots of men were gingery. Red hair —it was too vague, but it was something, and he knew about it. Did it matter how he had come to know about it? Perhaps he could ring up and still be honest—say something like "I have reason to believe the assailant had red hair, was young, of medium height," and so on, but would the police leave it there? He doubted it. They would surely dig and ferret away, knowing as indeed he himself did that a list of characteristics was not enough. To say red hair was not enough. You had to demonstrate, as Sylvia had, how the hair grew upward in a quiff. It was not enough to say the man moved furtively; you had to be able to show just how he had moved. Identification by an eyewitness was certainly what was needed. Only Sylvia could give them that, and she was not in a position to do so. Full circle.

At lunchtime Terence couldn't face going to the canteen. He sent out for coffee and a fresh pack of cigarettes and moved over to the window. Down below, the newsboys were shouting out the early editions of the evening papers. Terence found himself wishing passionately that they were announcing the arrest of the man who attacked girls, but the birdlike cries rising through the fog and the traffic were all about football. The police made no statement at all that day, and in the evening Sylvia rang again and said she was coming round to the flat.

Terence waited for her in a state of tension, and she gave him no quarter. "Have you seen the evening papers?" she began before the door was fairly closed. "They say that girl's condition is serious."

"She'll recover then," he said. Sylvia frowned at him. "Serious, fair, grave—that's the way it goes in descending order. Serious, you'll recover, fair, you have a chance, grave, you've had it."

"Need you be so flippant?" she said. He had never felt less flippant in his life.

She went on talking, urgently, obsessively, but he had

stopped listening. It was as though he was gathering himself together, like a horse before a leap, all his thoughts and feelings coiling down tightly before exploding into action. "All right," he said, interrupting her in midsentence. "What's the number?"

She was taken completely unaware. "You mean you're going to ring the police?" she asked uncertainly, thinking she must have misunderstood him.

"Yes. What's the number?" he repeated impatiently. Really, she looked almost stupid, her face puddingy with shock.

"I don't know offhand," she said nervously. "It'll be in the book under Police, won't it? You mean you're going to ring now?"

But Terence was already looking through the directory, too preoccupied to answer her. Carrying the book, his finger on the listed number, he went across to the telephone and she ran around the couch and put her hand on his arm. "Are you ringing the police right now?" she cried again.

"Why not?" he said, dialing.

"But you haven't thought about what to say!" she protested. Standing right beside him, she could hear the phone ringing at the other end and panic swept through her. She wanted him to put the phone down immediately, before anyone answered, before they were involved. "Wait!" she cried, but it was too late, someone was speaking, and then Terence, crisp and cool, was giving his name and address, stating his business. Sylvia closed her eyes for an instant. They were committed.

Terence put the phone down and turned to face her. "They're sending someone around right away," he said.

"From the police station?" she cried. "The one just up in the High Street? But they'll be here any minute. I can't stay here with them coming." Frantically she caught up her coat, grabbed her handbag.

"Wait a minute," he said. "What's the mad rush? There's no need to run away. Just go into the bedroom while they're here, why don't you? They'll only be a few minutes."

"Hide in the bedroom, with the police just through the door?" she exclaimed. "What if I sneezed?"

Terence laughed but Sylvia was quite serious and already pulled the door open. "I hope I don't meet them on the stairs," she said.

"Look, Sylvia," he said, hurrying after her, "if you leave now I can't come with you. I mean, I've got to be here when they arrive, otherwise it would look queer seeing I told them it was all right to come straight on round—"

"That's all right," she interrupted, hurrying down, intent only on getting away. "Ring me tomorrow, let me know how it went." She was gone out into the street without a backward glance.

He went back to his living room and watched from the window as she fled across the square. She disappeared round the corner but he was still standing at the window looking after her when a police car turned into the square from the opposite direction and cruised slowly along the curb before stopping outside the block of flats. Two men in the front seat, one in the back. As Terence watched, the front passenger jumped smartly out and opened the rear door. The other passenger emerged from the back seat. He was not in uniform, and Terence felt excitement, mingled with apprehension. A senior officer had come to hear what he had to say;

31

they were treating his call seriously. The men stepped across the pavement, leaving the driver at the wheel, and Terence heard their heavy tread on the stairs. After a moment's hesitation, he opened his door and stood waiting for them.

"I saw your car," he said in explanation.

They were most correct. The older one introduced himself as Inspector Quirke and looked around. "It's a nice flat you have, sir," he said politely, almost deferentially. "Do you live here on your own?"

This simple question unsettled Terence. As he answered, he caught himself looking for traces of Sylvia's recent presence. He had a distinct and unpleasant sensation of having been put on the wrong foot at the very start of the interview.

The inspector made a few more remarks of a social nature, then apparently feeling he had satisfied the conventions, he launched into the purpose of his visit.

"Now, Mr. Lambert," he began, "you say that on the night of Tuesday the sixteenth of January you saw a girl being attacked in the street outside your residence. Is that correct?"

Here it was, the big lie. Once it was spoken the rest would follow more easily. "Yes," he said. "That's right."

"You were looking out of this window when you saw the attack?" said the inspector, walking over to it.

"Yes."

"You were looking out of the window and you just happened to see the girl walking along?"

"Yes, that's right," said Terence again.

"You had the light on and the curtains drawn back?"

"No, actually the light was off."

"So you were standing in the dark looking out of the window?"

"Not really," said Terence, beginning to sweat. "As a matter of fact I was in bed, and then I got up and happened to pull back the curtain a bit. I looked out of the window and saw the girl and this man."

"Was there anything that made you look out?"

"How do you mean, made?"

"Well, you may have heard footsteps running, or even the girl screaming, something like that."

"No, I didn't hear anything."

"So you just happened to look out of the window, for no particular reason?"

"That's what I said, I happened to look out." *Steady now. Hell, why had Sylvia been gazing out the window? There may have been a noise of some kind. He should have asked her.*

"Just getting the picture, sir. Now, if you wouldn't mind telling us what you saw when you looked out."

Terence began cautiously, realizing for the first time how many pitfalls lay ahead of him. He had been in too much of a hurry, he should have got Sylvia to brief him, to go over and over the details with him. "The girl was walking along the far side of the square," he said.

"Did you know her?" asked the inspector.

"No, of course I didn't know her," said Terence irritably. "I'd never seen her before."

"Go on."

"She was a young girl, oh, in her teens, and she had long blond hair hanging straight down. She was wearing a miniskirt, some bright color, orange I'd say, and she was carrying some sort of bag. She had on one of those suede jackets, imitation suede I suppose, and boots."

"Color of the jacket, sir?"

"Oh, brown." At least Sylvia had described the girl fully; he could afford to be absolutely positive at this stage of the interview.

"In which direction was she walking?"

"From left to right. From there to about there, while I was watching," said Terence, pointing.

"And where was the girl when you first noticed the man?"

Careful now. "About halfway along. Then I saw this man coming after her."

"Running?"

What was it Sylvia had said? "Sort of gliding along, but fast."

"Did it occur to you that he was pursuing the girl?"

"Not at first. I thought he was out on a training run. He had on these gym shoes, and a track suit. He looked like an athlete."

"Gym shoes, sir?"

"Canvas, with rubber soles. Plimsolls, white ones, and the track suit was dark. Black, I think, though it's hard to be sure under the lights."

"Go on, sir."

"He caught up with the girl, got right behind her, that is, and then instead of going on past her as I expected him to do, he, well, he pounced on her, got her by the throat."

"And what did you do, sir?"

"Do?"

"Did you bang on the window? Shout?"

"I think I did. I'm not sure," said Terence, unable to decide quickly which was the safest answer. "It all happened so quickly, I could hardly believe my eyes. I mean, one minute everything was perfectly normal, and then this. Anyhow the girl screamed as soon as he touched her and people came running from all directions."

"You didn't think of ringing the police at the time?"

"I thought someone else would, one of the people who actually talked to the girl afterward. Didn't anybody ring?"

"If someone did, we'll have a record of it," said the inspector.

"I wonder if anyone else actually saw the man," said Terence. The inspector said nothing, and Terence was forced to answer himself. "I don't suppose so," he said. "He made off as soon as the girl screamed."

"Is there anything else you'd care to add?" asked the inspector.

"I don't think so," said Terence.

"Nothing else about the man's appearance?"

"He was young, I'd say, rather thin, average height, about my build, in fact. A good bit smaller than you, Inspector, or the sergeant here, but the way he was moving, he looked quite fit."

"Anything else, sir?"

Damnation, almost as if he knew Terence was holding something back! "Well," he said reluctantly, "at the time I was pretty sure he had red hair."

"At the time? Does that mean you've changed your mind?"

"Not exactly. It's just that it's weeks ago now; I'm not quite so sure about it, that's all."

"But you still *think* the man had red hair?"

"Yes, that's right, I think he had."

"Thank you, sir," said the inspector. "Sergeant Jessup here will type his notes up when he gets back to the station. Perhaps you could call in and sign the statement sometime in the next day or two. After you've read it through, of course."

Out in the car the inspector said to the sergeant, "I think we're on to something here."

"Sir?" said the sergeant.

"What Lambert says ties in with what we know already from the people who came out to help the girl. And then his description of the girl is pretty accurate. There's no doubt he saw her. He's got the clothes right and everything. But the most interesting thing from our point of view is that one of the crank letters mentioned red hair, black track suit and white gym shoes—called them that too."

"Do you think, sir, it was Mr. Lambert who wrote that letter?"

"It's certainly possible, but somehow I don't think so. No reason to, as far as I can see."

The sergeant glanced across at the inspector. The old man looked quite mild, even benevolent. Sergeant Jessup decided to risk a further comment. "Mr. Lambert was a bit nervous, wouldn't you say?" he asked.

"Doesn't mean a thing. Nine people out of ten are jumpy when they're talking to the police."

"Yes, sir," said the sergeant, but he said it doubtfully. "I'd have said, though, that Lambert was a smooth type. Not one to be rattled easily, I'd have thought."

Back in the flat Terence was thinking it had gone off not so badly. He went over what had been said, and there was only one thing that made him uneasy. He wished he had not mentioned red hair. That detail bothered him. It was too pat, somehow. He kept on remembering that Sylvia had not said anything about the man's hair until days after the incident, when she was trying desperately to convince him that she had seen the man quite clearly, clearly enough to be able to identify him. As an experiment, Terence stationed himself at his window and kept watch for twenty minutes on end. It was a night like the other night, dark and cold, with the same streetlights shining away in the murk. He saw seventeen people pass, well wrapped up against the weather, and he could not have sworn as to the color of the hair of any one of them.

Nevertheless, he called at the police station the next day and signed the statement, red hair and all. Having gone so far, there seemed nothing else he could do.

Once Terence had contacted the police and made his statement, everything returned to normal as suddenly and completely as if he had thrown a switch. Even the girl in the hospital was pronounced out of danger. Sylvia, glowing with relief and gratitude, was as charming as she had ever been. Her family, with no suppressed tension on her part to unsettle them, were placid and cheerful again and so incurious that Sylvia risked going to the flat on three nights during the week that followed.

Terence had been to the police station to sign on Wednesday. Saturday of the following week Edgar was to give a paper at a weekend school of business administration. He had been flattered when they asked him and in his usual methodical manner he had worked on the paper and had finished it in good time. Once he was satisfied with it he relaxed and began to look on the whole weekend as a treat. The course was being held in a large house set in beautiful grounds in the depths of the country. Edgar was traveling down by train, but he was to be met at the station and driven to the house in time for luncheon. His talk, which was set down for two-thirty, was to be followed by a discussion, then tea with the students. Edgar had been promised a visit to some interesting local ruins after tea, and there was to be a formal dinner with distinguished fellow guests. A fast train would get him back to town about midnight. Altogether it promised to be an unusually civilized occasion for Edgar, whose only regular outings were to the monthly meetings of the local branch of the Society of Accountants and occasionally to tepid social functions connected with his work when he felt obliged to attend.

Sylvia was pleased for him. She searched out his evening clothes, hardly worn for years, and made him try them on. They fitted—he had put on no weight—but she took them in to be cleaned and pressed. On Friday afternoon she was folding them and putting them in a suitcase for him to take with him when the girls came into the bedroom and reminded her that they too would be away all the next day, playing in a hockey tournament. Sylvia immediately decided that she would spend this unexpectedly free day with Terence, and never mind the risks. Their last meeting outside the flat had ended badly, they had quarreled, and they had been seen together by that friend of Julie's, but Sylvia was in the mood to forget all that. She was feeling gay and relaxed, and in a way invincible. The fact that the police had been told about the man with red hair and nothing had come of it gave Sylvia the heady sensation that the two of them were having their cake and eating it too. They had confessed, they had cleared their consciences, yet they had not had to endure any unpleasant consequences, perform any penance.

38

That the confessing had been done by Terence was a small point that Sylvia found easy to overlook. Indeed, as the days passed, it increasingly seemed to her that she herself had done something praiseworthy, something that deserved a reward, and the prospect of spending a whole long day with Terence away from the flat and the town presented itself to her as a perfectly splendid way of celebrating the end of all their worries.

She lost no time in telephoning Terence and telling him what she had in mind. It was a fine evening, the next day promised to be fine too. Terence was delighted at the thought of driving through the countryside and seeing the first signs of spring with Sylvia at his side. He no longer owned a car, had sold his, in fact, after his affair with Sylvia had developed to the point where he found he was spending most of his free time at home, but he hired the smartest little car he could find, put blankets and cushions in the trunk, a flashlight, a transistor radio, a box of chocolates, a book of maps in the glove compartment. As an afterthought he added a silver flask of brandy. He enjoyed having a car again, consciously pretended to himself that it was really his, deliberately shut out the fact that the car and the woman alike were his just for the day. On Saturday he woke early, shaved and dressed with care, made himself breakfast, then sat and smoked and waited for the phone to ring, grudging every wasted minute of the bright day.

At the Mansons', the girls left to catch their bus immediately after breakfast. As soon as Edgar too was safely away Sylvia rang Terence to say she was on her way, then ran upstairs to put on her suede coat and fur hat. She knotted her prettiest scarf at her throat, then hurried along to the corner where Terence was to pick her up. Quick as she had been, he was there before her. She stepped into the roadster gaily, like a young girl, and they headed west out of town. They were in tearing good spirits, their hopes were high. They were not disappointed. It proved to be one of those enchanted days when everything goes right. The sun shone, the birds sang, the roads were reasonably free of traffic. When they were ready to eat they found the most perfect place, where they sat by an open fire and ate jugged hare, a storybook dish which neither of them had ever tasted before, followed by black currant tart and thick country cream. Later they drove down a lane where the high banks were already starred with primroses. Terence took out the blankets and cushions, and they left the car and walked a little way into the woods. Where there was an open, dry space they spread the blankets carefully before lying down in each other's arms. Afterward, when they were still, Sylvia saw above Terence's head a robin, still red-breasted from the winter, perched upon a thorny twig and outlined against the clear pale blue of the sky. She smiled dreamily up at him, fancying he was watching over them.

Julie and Marion were due home at six, but Sylvia persuaded Terence to stop for tea on the way back to town. "It doesn't matter if I'm still out when they get home," she said. "On such a lovely afternoon I could easily have been walking in the park."

That was in fact what she did tell her daughters when she walked in late, radiant and sparkling, and they seemed to accept what she said as the truth.

Terence, like Edgar, was an accountant, a fact which Sylvia found amusing. It intrigued her that the two men in her life should have the same qualifications and yet have used them as the basis for such utterly different careers. Edgar had joined his firm straight from school as a junior clerk, had studied and taken examinations for years, staying in nights and weekends to do it, and was now a senior accountant with prospects of ending up as assistant chief accountant—someone else was in line for the top job. Terence on the other hand had gained his qualifications with apparent ease, turning his hand to accountancy in his twenties when he came out of the army, and since then he had taken on a series of colorful jobs, open to someone quick with figures who knew his way around the tax laws. He had managed a pop group, been on overseas location with a television team, organized an angry young charity group, been involved with a flamboyant entrepreneur who had subsequently gone bankrupt and killed himself, and was currently trying to sort out the affairs of a small business that made ladies' gloves.

It all made Edgar's steady, slow progress up the rungs seem frightfully tame. Sylvia, however, was always quick to remind herself that Terence could afford to take risks, whereas Edgar, married, with children, with no money apart from his salary, could not. Terence had a private income, a few hundred pounds a year. For Sylvia, this was part of his charm. When, right at the beginning, he had told her he had money of his own, this had invested him with glamour in her eyes. No one else she knew had a private income; because of it she imagined him moving in more sophisticated circles than her other acquaintances, belonging to a different, suaver world. The money had been left to Terence by his father, an Indian Army officer who had retired before Terence was born to a small holding in Ireland. He had fathered Terence, his only child, at fifty-five, and had died aged seventy-three in a hunting accident, leaving the whole of his estate to the boy.

Terence was doubly independent. On the one hand he had a steady, if small, income. On the other, he had no family responsibilities. He had once been married, but his wife had left him, after three years and no children, for a man who played the clarinet in an orchestra in Birmingham. After the first few months Terence had never heard from her again, and he had divorced her for desertion years before.

Yet in spite of his independence and his nonchalant disregard of the future Terence took each successive job seriously, and it was therefore quite in character, on the Sunday following his day in the country with Sylvia, for him to stay at home and to work on the glove factory's accounts. The work in fact absorbed him, and at two o'clock, when he realized he had had no lunch, he made himself a pot of coffee and some sandwiches and carried on.

When the phone rang at half past five, he answered it absentmindedly, his attention still on the papers in front of him, but the voice at the other end soon jerked him into watchful awareness.

"Detective Nicholson here," it was saying. "Is that Mr. Lambert?"

"Lambert speaking," said Terence and heard the guarded note in his own voice.

"Mr. Lambert, the inspector was wondering if you could attend an identification parade at the station this evening."

"This evening? But it's Sunday," said Terence, then immediately wondered how he could have said anything so stupid.

"All the same to us, sir," said the detective.

Terence pulled himself together. "An identification

parade," he said briskly, writing the word "parade" on a corner of the paper in front of him. "I expect it's in connection with that affair last month?"

"I expect so, sir." The detective was noncommittal.

"What time tonight?"

"Seven o'clock, sir."

Terence thought irritably that no one said "sir" as often as a policeman. "Seven o'clock at the station," he said aloud. "All right, I'll be there." He hung up and wrote "7 P.M." neatly under "parade," then pushed the papers away and lit a cigarette. He felt distinctly uneasy. To the best of his knowledge, for an identification parade several men would be lined up and he would be invited to inspect them and if possible to pick out the man he had seen. Which in his case was impossible. Right then he decided that he was simply not in a position to identify anybody. He had to go to the police station, he had to attend the parade. All right, he would go, he would look carefully at the men lined up for his inspection, and he would then state definitely that he had never to his knowledge seen any of the men before. This, after all, would be the truth. It was quite straightforward. It involved no lies, no deception. He would be absolutely in the clear, he could not be blamed for anything. It was routine, would take only five minutes, and at the end he would regretfully shake his head and that would be that.

Once he had thought the thing through, Terence felt quite cheerful but he was keyed up, on edge, and instead of going on with his work he cooked himself some bacon and eggs. By the time he had eaten them and tidied up it was half past six. He had a quick shave and walked down the road to the police station.

The man at the front desk had clearly been told to expect him. He came around and escorted Terence through to an inner room. Inspector Quirke was already there and waiting. There were handshakes, hearty greetings. Terence was being welcomed as a colleague, as an ally against the enemy. There was a treacherous atmosphere of bonhomie around. When they told him what they wanted him to do Terence found himself feeling sorry that he was going to disappoint them.

"The lads ready, sergeant?" asked the inspector, standing up.

"All there, sir," said the sergeant.

They went through to a narrow courtyard in single file, Terence in the middle. Lined up against a brick wall, facing strong lights, were about a dozen men, all in dark trousers and white shirts. Terence stopped abruptly at the threshold, trying to adjust to the situation. He had expected to see a lineup of men, but the sight of them there in front of him, so silent and so still, filled him with a most unexpected emotion—that of acute embarrassment. Useless to tell himself that all except one, or maybe even all of them, were ordinary citizens like himself, just helping the police out. Lined up so unnaturally, they looked sinister, alien. Terence felt that he and they were on different sides.

"That's right, sir, take your time," said the inspector behind him.

Thus prompted, Terence began to pace slowly along the row of men, with the policemen following behind, so closely he could hear their heavy breathing right behind his ear. He felt unreal, like an actor, but he examined each face carefully, as though he expected to recognize someone there.

The twelve men stared expressionlessly past him, anonymous, impossible to place. Policemen, postmen, professors, who could tell?

He came to a man with sandy hair and freckles. Was this the suspect, brought in by his reddish hair? But the hair was cut short, crew cut, and the man himself was square and stocky. Sylvia would never have described such a man as "gliding along." He was incapable of such a lissome motion, Terence was sure. He passed him by with a clear conscience. The next few were easy. Brown hair, fair hair, unusually tall and thin, too old . . . Terence, relieved, found himself moving with confident speed toward the end of the row. Then he came to the eleventh man— pale blue eyes on a level with his own, young and slim, with red hair springing strongly up from an unlined forehead. Terence felt a curious tingling shock. Here was the possibility he had failed to face up to, Sylvia's man come to life in nightmare flesh and blood. At almost the same instant he realized something else, perhaps even more shattering in its implications—this red-haired man was someone he had seen before, someone he had seen often, although he couldn't immediately place him. Mechanically, he kept moving, scrutinized the last man, allowed himself to be led a few yards away.

"Well?" asked the inspector.

There was no time to think out a new course of action. Terence shook his head quickly, instinctively. "No," he said, his voice sounding unexpectedly loud and clear to his own ears. "No, I'm afraid not, Inspector."

A tremor passed over Inspector Quirke's face—disappointment? exasperation?—but his voice was as smoothly deferential as before. "I see, sir," he said. "Perhaps you'd care to have another look?"

"Oh, I don't think so," said Terence, beginning to turn away, but the inspector was quietly insistent.

"It'll take only a couple of minutes," he said, and Terence passed unwillingly back along the line pretending to examine each man a second time, but letting his eyes slide quickly over the pale face of the man with red hair. Once more he shook his head, and this time they had to let him go.

Terence was deeply disturbed by what he considered the almost incredible turn of events. On the pavement outside the police station he realized that he had never really believed in Sylvia's red-haired assailant, and to be confronted in such circumstances by a man who corresponded at each point to her description was an unnerving experience. Then on top of that to find that he had actually met the man in question, that he was someone he ought to know! Was this man, whom he should recognize and whom Sylvia had described with uncanny accuracy, was this man the suspect, the one the police had expected him to identify? Terence's mind shied away from this terrifying possibility. It was too much; he clung to the hope that it was a coincidence. After all, a lot of people looked alike, especially people with red hair; there must be thousands of red-haired young men who were thin and pale. Terence worried in case the police had noticed the way he had reacted when he had come face to face with the man in the lineup, but surely they would have expected him to look closely at any man with red hair. In the absence of any positive identification, he was in the clear there, he was almost sure. Absolutely neutral, neither attracting suspicion to the man nor diverting it from him—that was the only line he could take.

Once he had settled this in his own mind, temporarily at least, his thoughts turned, reluctantly, even shrinkingly, to the other fantastic aspect of the matter, the fact that the man was known to him. He had seen him fairly often, he knew, the face was quite familiar to him, but the name eluded him. For a few groping minutes he could not even put him in context. He tried to work out where he had met him, where he belonged. Not in an office. Not in a shop. Was he perhaps a news agent, a bus conductor, a taxi driver? He was sure he was someone that he would recognize immediately in his usual environment. Was he the local postman, the barman at a nearby pub, maybe a waiter? Something like that, Terence was certain.

While he had been working at this problem of identity, he had been walking slowly along toward the flat. He waited at a corner for a car to pass and, the smell of exhaust fumes perhaps acting as a catalyst, memory performed its conjuring trick and presented him with a clear picture of the red-haired man in greasy mechanic's overalls. "Henderson," he said aloud, clicking his fingers.

As soon as the name came to him he was positive he was right. It was certainly young Henderson from the big garage in the High Street, Henderson's garage. This was the son of the owner. Terence had had dealings with both of them in the days when he owned his own car—months now since he had been up there, but he had known the father quite well and had taken a casual interest in the son. He remembered that young Henderson had worked on his car several times and he racked his brains for everything he could recollect about him, but all he could dredge up was an impression that the lad had been silent, even sullen, though a good enough mechanic.

Terence climbed the stairs to his flat, feeling that hours had passed since he left there, although it was not yet eight o'clock. He mixed himself a drink, then sat down and wondered what, if anything, he should do next. After a while, he remembered that Henderson's garage, whatever it called itself, was open twenty-four hours a day, seven days a week, which meant it would be open at that moment. Terence set his glass down with a thump. He admitted to himself that he had a powerful urge to go up right away, to reassure himself that things were normal by seeing father and son going about their lawful business. Out in the street it had begun raining, but he turned his collar up and trudged along the deserted roads up to the High Street. That was empty too, wet and shining under the powerful lights. The neon sign above the garage was visible from a block away, there was a notice outside that said "Open" and a light was shining through the glass door of the office; there was no other sign of life. Terence stood on the pavement opposite gazing at the line of petrol pumps and the closed door of the workshop. The rain fell diagonally, splashing into puddles on the asphalt, filling the gutters, seeping into his shoes. A car passed, then another. Neither of them drew into the garage forecourt. Terence had no idea what to do next. Without a car he could not demand service. They knew him there; he could hardly pretend he was lost and on such a night there was no opportunity of a casual approach. Terence crossed the road, going as close to the garage office as he dared, but he could see nothing at all through the steamy window. Finally, dissatisfied and chilled to the bone, he gave up and went home.

He woke up the following morning with a cold, and was embarrassed to think how he had caught it. His damp vigil of the night before seemed an aberration, a bad dream. He could hardly imagine himself doing such a senseless thing. He excused himself by blaming the strain of the identification parade and what he now believed was the coincidence of the man with red hair. He rang the office and said he would not be in, intending to nurse his cold in bed and do some more work on the factory accounts, but though he made himself comfortable with extra pillows and a board to write on, he made very slow progress. In the end he pushed all the papers aside, so that they fell on the floor, and huddled down miserably under the blankets. He badly wanted to ring Sylvia but first he had to decide how much he should tell her.

Meanwhile, Sylvia had enjoyed a peaceful Sunday with her family. She was more than ever convinced that her liaison with Terence indirectly benefited everyone she came into contact with. She was a better wife and mother because of him; he made her so happy, so relaxed and good-tempered, that the whole family basked in an atmosphere of well-being.

On this particular Sunday she took the girls breakfast in bed, then spent the rest of the morning preparing a traditional roast dinner. She also made Edgar's favorite lemon pudding. Perhaps responsive to her holiday feeling, Edgar brought the sherry decanter and glasses out to her in the kitchen and they sat companionably at the table there, chatting about the girls and the garden and their summer holiday plans. In the afternoon it was Sylvia's turn to read the Sunday papers while Edgar caught up on various odd jobs around the place. The girls offered to get the tea, and they sat around the fire and ate toasted sandwiches, which were Marion's specialty, and stuffed eggs, which were Julie's. Sylvia was glad to hear the girls chattering away so happily. She and Edgar had agreed that morning that Julie had been rather silent lately. Sylvia reflected that without the interludes with Terence, domestic days such as this one might seem dull; with more exciting occasions to provide color and contrast they seemed delightful. Contentment washed over her. It had been a good weekend, and Terence would ring in the morning.

In fact, it was evening before he rang, which was very awkward because Julie answered the phone. She came back looking extremely inquisitive, and said, "It's a man, for you, Mother. He didn't say his name."

Sylvia was immediately sure it was Terence. The telephone was out in the hall, and although she closed the living-room door before she picked up the receiver she was still conscious of the three of them just through the wall. She cut through Terence's first remarks and asked him to hold on while she went upstairs to the extension. She went up stealthily, hoping to avoid explanations to the family, took the receiver off, then ran down and replaced the other one. Only then, safely back on the upstairs landing, did she feel free to talk.

"What on earth have you been doing?" Terence demanded, when he had her back on the line.

"Don't be cross, darling, I've just been making things safe for us. That's all right, isn't it?"

"I suppose so," he said.

"Terence," she cried accusingly, "you've got a cold! Did you get it on Saturday?"

"Saturday?" he repeated.

She frowned at the blank note in his voice. "Yes," she said, "when we were, you know, out of the car."

"Of course I didn't catch it then!" He sounded positively hostile.

Sylvia decided to laugh it off. "At least you could have said that differently," she remarked, "like, 'How could I have caught cold on Saturday, darling, with you to keep me warm?'"

"As a matter of fact," said Terence, ignoring her teasing, "I got drenched to the skin last night."

"Did you fall into a duck pond or something?" she asked, like a pert girl.

"You seem to be determined to be funny tonight," said Terence.

"And you seem determined to be sorry for yourself," said Sylvia, with a flash of anger, but she checked herself, not wanting to precipitate a quarrel. "What were you doing then?" she asked instead, making herself sound as sympathetic as possible.

She was sure Terence hesitated for a minute. Then he said, "Oh, I had to go up to the High Street. Being Sunday night, there just weren't any taxis around so I had to walk up, and back again too. In case you don't know, it was pouring with rain."

"There's not much doing in the High Street on Sunday night," said Sylvia, fishing.

"You're dead right," said Terence. "Look, am I going to see you tomorrow?"

At that moment a door opened downstairs. "I'll be round about eight," said Sylvia quickly. "Hope you're better by then. Look, I can't talk any more just now, someone's coming. Till tomorrow." She put the receiver down quickly but quietly, and went through to her bedroom. When Marion looked in a minute later Sylvia had one of her drawers out.

"*There* you are," said her daughter. "What are you looking for?"

"A slip I was going to mend," said Sylvia.

"Who was that on the phone?"

"The phone? Oh, that was just someone from the club, wondering if I knew where the key to the property cupboard was." Really, the worst thing about an affair was all the grubby little lies you had to keep on telling, to your husband, of course, but also to your friends, your relations, your own children.

"Did you?" asked Marion.

"Did I what?"

"Know where the key was?"

"No," said Sylvia shortly. There was a limit to invention. She found the torn slip and brought her sewing downstairs, and the four of them watched television together in apparent harmony, but Sylvia's happy mood was quite spoiled. She hated to think she had lied to Marion, and she blamed Terence for it because he had rung at such an inconvenient time, quite forgetting how she had scolded him a few weeks before for not ringing when the family was at home. Also, when she went over their telephone conversation in her mind she was dissatisfied with it. Terence had been definitely bad-tempered, and she was sure he had deliberately avoided telling her why he had been out walking in the rain. Sylvia tried to think what could have taken him up the street but she was unable to think of a single reason. There were pubs and news agents nearer, the station was in another direction, if he had gone to the cinema surely he would have said. It was an irritating little mystery.

Meanwhile, Terence was just as annoyed with himself. He had intended to tell Sylvia about the identification parade, speaking of it lightly as an amusing experience, not mentioning the red-haired man as such but explaining that one of the men in the lineup had been from the local garage. Then he could have described his expedition up to the High Street and they could have laughed together at how he had stood staring at the place in the rain. But somehow her flippancy over the telephone had put him off. The whole thing had gone wrong, and when she had asked him point-blank what he had been doing out in the street he had clumsily avoided answering her question. He had muffed his chance and he now very much doubted whether he would ever be able to tell her about it in the casual way he felt was essential. Any hint of strain or worry, and he was sure she would panic, insist on taking some sort of precipitate action, be convinced of certainties where Terence himself saw only tenuous possibilities. It was all very difficult. Terence felt himself getting more and more caught up in a baffling web that was hampering his actions and distorting his outlook.

Sylvia knew nothing about the parade but she sensed something had happened to upset Terence, and she was uneasy. She discovered other worries too, now that her gay mood had evaporated. She tried not to think about the anonymous letter she had sent or about being seen that night by Julie's friend or about all the lies she was telling, but these and other matters now forced their way into her mind and made her increasingly nervous. The following evening, however, she made a determined effort to banish all disturbing thoughts, and she presented herself at Terence's door at eight o'clock with a bunch of grapes, three lemons and a girlie magazine. Terence accepted the role of an invalid with relief. To both of them it was a welcome explanation for his surliness of the previous day.

Sylvia bustled about the kitchen and made him a hot lemon drink and laced it with whisky, then drank half of it herself, because, she said, it smelled so nice and besides, prevention was at least as important as cure. She made Terence take a hot bath, being charmingly autocratic about it, and while he was out of the room she stripped his bed and changed his sheets and found an extra pillow in the closet to tuck behind his back. She then persuaded him to get back into bed, though of course in his condition there was no question of her joining him there this evening. Somehow with all this cosseting there was no time for serious talk. The atmosphere was wrong. It would have been like interrupting a children's game with incomprehensible adult worries.

Nevertheless, once Terence was tucked in bed with Sylvia sitting cozily beside him darning one of his socks—a thing she had never done before—he felt obliged to tell her the story he had concocted for his Sunday activities. He therefore embarked on a circumstantial tale of having promised to meet a chap in a pub and then realizing that by mistake he had told him the name of a pub in the High Street instead of the one near his flat that he had meant to say, and how he had not been able to get hold of him to explain his mistake so that he had been forced to walk all the way up to the High Street pub in the rain, only to find that by the time he got there the chap had got tired of waiting and had gone, so that there was nothing else for Terence to do except turn around and walk home again, still in the rain. Terence was proud of this story; it seemed to him to cover everything very neatly. Sylvia listened and smiled and nodded and didn't believe a word of it. Behind her calm, smiling, sympathetic face her thoughts were in a ferment. She was immediately certain Terence had been with a woman, had very likely met her in a pub and gone home with her, walking together arm in arm through the rain, escaping from loneliness and the deserted Sunday-evening streets into the warmth of a double bed. She imagined him coming reluctantly away from the woman, trudging back through the rain to his dark, chilly flat, and not ringing Sylvia herself up until late the following day and then only out of duty. Sylvia's thoughts, her emotions, seethed and bubbled, yet at the same time she felt very cool and alert, like a boxer in training, on the eve of a big fight which he expects to win but which he is not taking any chances about, just the same. She hid all this from Terence, made him supper before she left, and promised to come again on Friday.

She came as promised, in the late afternoon, when her family thought she was having tea with an elderly cousin of her mother's. She found Terence almost recovered. He had resolutely pushed the events of the previous Sunday to the back of his mind, telling himself that they were trivial and unimportant and not worth mentioning to Sylvia in the first place. What did they amount to, after all? A routine check, a pointless walk in the rain. These arguments together with his intervening illness effectively reduced the whole business to something dim and far away. The identification parade was like a dream sequence, his trek up to the garage a fragment of nightmare. He now had no desire whatsoever to talk to Sylvia about any of it. All he wanted to do was to enjoy Sylvia as greedily as possible.

For her part, Sylvia had come determined to exorcise the other woman. She had thought about her a great deal in the preceding few days and had come to some definite conclusions about her. She was sure, for one thing, that she was a woman without encumbrances, able to come and go, free to drink in a pub on a Sunday evening without having to think about a family meal. Free to invite a man home with her, free to visit a man in his flat at any time, without making excuses or telling lies to anybody. The thought of a woman having that sort of freedom made Sylvia quite sick with envy. Men had it, of course, Terence had it, but for some reason Sylvia had come to assume that all other women were like her, hemmed in with responsibilities and conventions. She had forgotten there were untrammeled women still in the world.

And with these thoughts came the realization that though because of the demands of husband and family she herself could barely manage one affair, Terence had plenty of time and opportunity to indulge in several simultaneous liaisons. She saw him on the average two evenings a week; that left him with five free evenings, plus lunch hours, weekends, late afternoons (perfect for assignations over tea or cocktails). Say ten hours a week with her, against one hundred and fifty-eight hours without. It hardly bore thinking of, and to calculate that he spent ten hours with her was to be optimistic. He could have her on the side, as it were, and hardly notice it.

To her surprise, ever since Monday Sylvia had been consumed with jealousy. She was humiliated as well as surprised. She had been so confident that her relationship with Terence was under control, that she could take him or, if necessary, gracefully leave him alone, that she had been completely unprepared for the violence of her feelings when she sensed that their relationship was threatened and vulnerable. She was extremely hostile toward the other, unknown woman. Terence was hers; she was damned if she would let anyone else walk off with him. She approached his flat and his bed determined to blot the other woman completely out of his mind. Terence's mood matched hers. He had been worried, he had been ill, and now he wanted to put all that behind him and lose himself in his mistress. They came together and made love with an intensity they had never before achieved.

Yet afterward they each sensed a reserve in the other. It was as though the secrets they were keeping from each other were stealthily forming a barrier between them, impalpable and slight as yet, but menacing, like the first faint wisps of a mist destined to thicken to a fog which would eventually blot out all familiar landmarks.

"I hope you don't mind, sir. I took a chance of finding you at home." It was Saturday afternoon, and Inspector Quirke was on the doorstep. "I always seem to catch up with you on the weekend, don't I?"

"Has anything happened?" asked Terence. He felt extremely tense, although his apprehension was mingled with a hope that the inspector brought good news.

The inspector, however, shook his head. "I'm afraid not, though in a way it's just as well, seeing what could have happened."

"You mean another attack?"

"It's on the cards, isn't it?"

"Have you come about another parade, then?"

"Well, there wouldn't be much point in that, would there, Mr. Lambert?"

The inspector's look was very knowing. Terence knew he should brazen it out, ask what he meant, but he was afraid the inspector's answer might bring things to a head, and he badly wanted to avoid any sort of cards-on-the-table chat until he saw things a bit more clearly. When the inspector realized Terence was not going to say anything, he gave a small cough and suggested that they should both just step inside for a minute. "Not that I'll be keeping you long, sir, but we might as well be comfortable and private."

Once in the living room, he sank down on the divan with a sigh of evident relief. "That's better," he said. "It's not only the man on the beat that needs to get his feet up, you know."

"I suppose not," said Terence. The inspector, established on his couch, was now his guest. "Would you like a drink?"

"Not just now, thank you." The inspector spoke politely, even deferentially, but Terence felt he had been reproved for failing to appreciate the nature of the occasion. Policemen on duty did not drink. He himself badly wanted something to steady him, if not a whisky, then a cigarette. He offered the pack to Inspector Quirke, but the inspector shook his head again.

"I gave it up five years ago," he said.

In normal circumstances Terence could have taken up this remark and used it as the cue for several minutes of relaxed chat. As it was he simply could not think of a thing to say. In the presence of Inspector Quirke small talk just dried up and died. As if he realized this himself the inspector gave up any pretense of light conversation and came straight to what evidently was the point.

"I'll be frank with you, Mr. Lambert," he said, gazing across at Terence with an air of great candor which immediately put Terence even more on his guard. "We're not making much progress in this matter."

"I'm sorry to hear that," said Terence, speaking the literal truth. He was sorry to hear it. At that moment he was convinced he had never wanted anything half so much as a quick solution to this nightmare case.

"It's a matter of not having anything to go on," said the inspector. "Nothing positive, that is. No definite clues. Very little evidence of any kind. None of the girls saw his face at all, you know. He came creeping up behind them every time and then, pow! he was on them. But of course there's no need to tell *you* this, Mr. Lambert. You saw it all for yourself. In fact, between you and me, you're the only decent witness we've got, which is really why I'm here."

"But the attack I saw wasn't a serious one," said Terence. "It was hardly an attack at all. I mean, the man just touched her and she screamed and he ran away."

"She had bruises on her throat. Scratches too. And shock. Serious enough."

"Still, it's not like murder. Not as if I'd seen the actual murder."

"We think the two incidents are connected. I'd almost go as far as to say we're sure there is a connection. And as I said, that's why I'm here. What I'd like to do is to go over your statement again with you. Unless you have any objection?"

The inspector's shrewd cold eyes were on him. "No, no, of course not," Terence said. "Anything to help."

"Thank you very much indeed, sir," said the inspector, with what Terence regarded as excessive gratitude. He then very quickly got down to business and took Terence backward and forward through his story until the few sparse points it contained began to look positively threadbare. Terence wished he knew more about police procedure. Was this persistent questioning, this going over and over the same ground, just routine? Or was it that his statement rang false? Meeting the inspector's eyes, Terence was sure that the policeman knew he was lying, and he was afraid. To his own ears his story was less convincing each time he told it. He had been in bed in a darkened room, he had happened to get up and look out of the window at the very moment when a girl was being assaulted, he had not shouted, or gone to her help, or rung the police—he had not done anything at all for weeks, and then he had contacted the police and had made a statement alleging that this man whom he had seen only once, at night, at a distance, weeks before had had red hair and had worn white gym shoes. It was not good enough. He almost felt like apologizing for offering the inspector such a poor effort.

But then the seesaw began to go up again. Perhaps the inspector was not really suspicious of him at all. Perhaps to a policeman his statement seemed quite normal and believable. Maybe witnesses often behaved in the way he was behaving. He just did not know.

When the interview was over and he was showing the inspector out he said twice over that he was sorry he had not been more help, and he just stopped himself from saying it a third time. So much repetitious babbling was too clear a sign of strain.

The inspector, however, was philosophical, or apparently so, in a cracker-barrel sort of way. "That's the way it goes," he said. "What we need now is a lucky break. There are a lot of cases like this one, you know. Nothing happens for days and even weeks, you don't seem to be getting anywhere. Nothing jells, so to speak, and then one day, sometimes quite by accident, the right fact comes to light and when it's fitted into place, everything makes sense. I have the feeling this is going to be one of those cases. In the meantime, all we can do is to keep on looking. Well, we'll be seeing you, Mr. Lambert."

You probably will, at that, thought Terence as he shut the door. He was uneasy and depressed. Unless the inspector was being less than frank, the police inquiries were not going at all well. There was no early prospect of the killer being identified and caught, and until that happened he would not be able to relax and live normally. He mixed himself a drink that he had been inhibited from having while the inspector had been there, and sat down to think things out.

It was true that he was very much in the dark over the whole affair. He did not know what the police knew, he had no way of telling what they were thinking or what leads they were following up. On the other hand, when he thought about it, he realized he had a card in his hand that they could not have and could not know for certain that he had. That gave him one line of inquiry that he could follow up independently, one chance of getting at the truth before everything went to pieces. He knew that the man in the identification parade corresponded closely to the description that Sylvia had given him, and he also knew who that man was and where he lived. No doubt the police knew this last part too, but they had only Terence's own description to go on, and he had not identified the man or picked him out in any way.

61

As the police could not know his reasons, his failure to identify the man must have shaken any suspicions they had had
about him and might even have dissuaded them from making any further inquiries about him. Terence, however, knew
there was no reason for ruling him out, that there was in fact
every good reason for investigating him more closely. Terence also knew who he was and where he worked. It should
not be impossible for him to ferret out enough facts either to
implicate him further or to eliminate him completely.

For all the past week Terence had avoided thinking about
the red-haired Henderson. The memory of the identification
parade disturbed him, the recollection of his trek up to the
garage in the rain embarrassed him. He had pushed both
incidents to the back of his mind. But now Henderson's im-
age presented itself forcibly to him and in the interval it
seemed to have swollen in size and become more formidable.
There was no longer any question of ignoring it; indeed Terence was seized with an overwhelming desire to find out
more about this man and a crazy idea came into his mind.
Wondering at himself only a little, he rang the car-rental firm
and booked a car for that evening.

He went straight around to collect it, and when he found
it was the same car that he had hired to take Sylvia to the
country, he hardly registered the irony, being absolutely intent on his present plan, which was simple enough, but the
only one he could think of. He intended to drive straight up
to Henderson's garage and under cover of buying petrol to
try to get some information about the son who worked there
as a mechanic. To his extreme annoyance, however, he found
that the car-hire firm had filled the tank to the brim before
handing the car over. This, he remembered too late, was

their usual practice. He could not think of an alternative plan, so in order to use the petrol up he began to drive fast and aimlessly round and round squares, along arterial roads, cutting across commons, doubling back on his tracks, but the gauge remained maddeningly high. At last he bought a length of hose in a gardening shop miles from home, clumsily hacked off a short piece and feeling like a criminal, siphoned petrol out of the tank into the gutter of a side street.

Passing children stopped and watched him. "That's petrol, ain't it?" one asked.

"Someone put sugar in it," said Terence recklessly.

He went round to look at the gauge through the window and nearly panicked when it showed empty, then remembered it would not register anything until the engine was switched on. He turned the key and the needle swung slowly till it reached the quarter mark. Enough.

The children watched him closely as he screwed the cap on. "Do you think it'll start, mister?" asked the same boy. "Even wiv the sugar, like?"

Terence nodded tersely, being too strung up to speak, and slammed the door. The car leaped forward and when Terence looked in the mirror he saw the children staring after him. He had to remind himself that he had done nothing wrong, either then or earlier. He looked at his watch. Five-thirty; this absurd business with the petrol had cost him nearly two hours already, and he must be twelve or fifteen miles away from the garage. The evening rush had started; all the roads to the west were clogged with cars heading for the suburbs and home; the opposite lanes were crammed with cars coming back to town from a day in the country. The long metal snakes of traffic writhed and twisted, stopped and started and stopped again. Trapped in the queue, Terence watched the time and the petrol gauge and swore aloud. He began to lose confidence in his scheme. How could he spin out the purchase of a few gallons of petrol for long enough to learn anything at all about Henderson? (He must find out the chap's first name, that was one thing.) The police had it easy, he thought bitterly. They could just knock on the door and ask the questions directly. "Where were you on the night of the sixteenth of January? Do you have a black track suit? Do you wear white plimsolls?" They could question his family, his workmates. "Have you noticed anything odd about his behavior lately? Has he been out a lot at nights? Has he a steady girl friend? Has he ever been in trouble?" Terence thought of the questions and longed to know the answers.

At last he was able to get off the main road and cut through to the High Street. As he turned into it, the light on the dashboard came on, showing that the tank was nearly empty. He pulled up at the garage alongside the pumps and with some thought of prolonging the transaction got out of the car and stood beside it. He was uncomfortably tense, knowing that if he lost this chance of finding out something it would be hard to think of the next move.

An attendant came out, not either of the Hendersons, not anyone that Terence could remember seeing before.

"Fill her up," Terence said, but then he remembered he would be returning the car in a couple of hours. "Wait a minute," he said. "Just give me three gallons of the regular." This affair was costing him quite enough already.

When the petrol was in he asked the man to check the water and the oil, then the tires, trying to gain time, hoping one of the Hendersons would appear. No one came, though, and as he was paying Terence said in desperation, "Have you still got that red-haired chap working here?"

The man finished counting out his change and then gave some thought to the subject. "Do you mean Chris?" he said at last.

"Chris?"

"Chris Henderson."

"I don't know about names," said Terence. "Henderson—that's the boss, isn't it? This'll be his boy, then? Has he got red hair?"

"I'll say," said the man.

"That's probably him then," said Terence. "Is he around? I'd like a word if he is."

"He'll be out the back, working on the cars. Go through the lube bay and give him a shout."

Terence moved the car around the corner away from the pumps, then got out and went through to the workshop. The place looked deserted. A bright light was shining on one of the cars, which had its hood up, but the rest of the shed was in darkness. Terence hesitated, fighting an impulse to leave, but then he forced himself to go a few steps forward.

"Wanting something?" said a voice so close behind him that he jumped. He turned, and there he was, the man he was looking for, the wiry frame draped in mechanic's overalls, the red hair darkened with grease, the pale eyes noticeable in the grimy face.

"Yes," Terence said, making an effort to appear matter-of-fact. "My name's Lambert. You did some work on my car a while back. Changed the wheels around and fixed a rattle in a hub cap."

"What make of car was it?"

"Morris 1100," said Terence. "Dark green." So far he had told the truth. Now invention had to take over. "I sold the car a while ago and just this morning I had a ring from the chap who bought it. He says the jack's missing. I wondered if you'd come across it."

"How do you mean?"

"Well, I thought it might be lying around here somewhere. I mean to say it could have been left out, couldn't it, when you were working on the car?"

"No jack's been found here," said Henderson.

Careful now, a mistake to antagonize him. "I wonder," he said diffidently, "but are you sure? I mean, I didn't use the jack at all after you had the car in here. It was only two or three weeks later that I sold it, and I just assumed it was in the box in the boot where it had always been. I suppose you used it when you changed the wheels, didn't you?"

"I might have. Mostly we use our own jack."

"And you don't remember whether you had it out or not? Well, there it is, my jack's missing." He expected Chris Henderson to shrug and walk away and was surprised and encouraged to see he was prepared to discuss the matter a bit further. His tale about the jack must have been plausible, for Henderson was rubbing his chin and giving the matter some thought. "When did you say you brought the car in?" he asked after a moment.

Terence suddenly saw a way of forcing things. "Middle of January," he said, keeping his voice casual. "You had it for a couple of days. I brought it in on a Tuesday, I remember. Yes, that's right, Tuesday the sixteenth of January, not that I suppose the exact date matters to you." He was watching the other's face carefully. Did the pale eyes flicker, or was he imagining things? He decided to apply a little more pressure. "Now I come to think of it, you said you'd work late, have it ready for me in the morning. I needed it the next day but when I rang in the morning you said it wouldn't be ready till the afternoon."

"Yeah?" said the mechanic. "Can't say I remember the job."

"I daresay something cropped up, stopped you working on the car that night." He paused, but there was no reaction from the other. The excitement of the chase was building up in Terence. He could not resist another probing question. "I expect you work late pretty often?"

"Often enough."

"Bit creepy here on your own, isn't it?" But this time Henderson did not answer, and Terence was made to feel he had gone too far. "Well, if you do come across the jack perhaps you could ring me," he said, retreating. "My name's Lambert." He wrote his name and telephone number down and handed the slip of paper over. "You're Henderson, aren't you?" he went on, screwing his face up in a pretense of remembering. "Son of the owner?"

Chris Henderson nodded, then said unexpectedly, "That chap probably lost the jack himself. Putting you on, like."

"Could be," said Terence, relieved that the jack was all young Henderson seemed to be thinking of. Relieved and yet deflated too at the thought of all his careful, loaded questions missing their mark.

Back in the car he wondered if he had achieved anything at all. There had certainly been no dramatic reaction to any of his needling remarks, yet he was almost sure that when he mentioned the date there had been a change of expression, a slight tremor of awareness. But then, with a thump of his heart, he remembered the identification parade. Guilty or innocent, Chris Henderson must surely have known what that had been for, therefore mention of the sixteenth of January must have brought the murder to mind. Then came another, most unwelcome thought—Terence had recognized Henderson; as a corollary Henderson had no doubt recognized him, if not at the time then surely this evening. He could hardly have forgotten the face of someone who had inspected him at close quarters only a week before. Terence realized with dismay that in mentioning the date so deliberately he may have given away far more than he had gained.

Which raised another question. Surely an innocent man, a man with nothing to hide, would have referred to the parade, would have mentioned having seen Terence there, would have commented on it in some way; Henderson had said nothing at all. When he thought of it, though, Terence realized it would be unwise to read too much into this silence. Chris Henderson was naturally surly, not given to light conversation. It would be in character for him to refrain deliberately from mentioning any earlier contact. That Henderson had kept quiet was a fact; Terence could only guess at his reasons for doing so. This conclusion was depressing, and Terence gave an impatient sigh. Detective work was turning out to be damned difficult.

All the same, he had no intention of giving up yet for a while. It was better to be doing something, better even to be trying to do something, than to be sitting at home biting his nails, which he knew only too well was the alternative. He sat on in the car for a few minutes, then thought of another angle he could explore. He got out again and walked round to the front of the garage, where the owner's name was printed: "T. K. Henderson." Terence made a note of the initials, then drove till he saw a phone box. It was quite likely that the Hendersons had no telephone—three out of four households hereabouts managed without. There were, however, columns of Hendersons listed, dozens of C. Hendersons, but not to worry, for some reason Terence was sure Chris Henderson was unmarried and living at home, and, his first piece of luck that day, there was actually a T. K. Henderson listed and living in the general area. Terence found the street on a map and drove there immediately, without stopping to consider what he would do once he got there.

It turned out to be a quiet street, with a grass lawn and trees on each side. All the houses were the same, brick, semidetached, with a small front yard, a hedge and a gate. Number 23, the Hendersons' place, had absolutely nothing to distinguish it from any of the others. It was neither shabby nor aggressively neat, there was nothing distinctive about its paintwork or its garden or its front door, those three great suburban differentiators. It was completely average, and at this hour of the night the front curtains were all tightly drawn and there was no sign of life at all. This was true of all the houses. Terence imagined all the inhabitants crouched in front of TV sets in back rooms. Once he had taken all this in, he restarted the engine and drove slowly past the house. About fifty yards on he turned the car and parked it facing the house but on the other side of the street. He wanted to see when, and if, Chris Henderson came home, always supposing this was his home.

He expected to have to wait a long time, but it was barely

half an hour later when a car turned into the road and stopped outside number 23. Straining his eyes, Terence saw someone get out, run up the steps and let himself in. Terence was sure it was Chris Henderson. He felt now that he would never mistake that wiry figure, even in the dark and at a distance. The front door shut behind him with a kind of finality and the house remained in absolute darkness. Terence remembered that Henderson had taken the time to lock his car. It seemed unlikely that he would be going out again. It was ten-forty, he had promised to return the rental car by eleven. He started the engine and drove slowly back to the depot. He now knew young Henderson's Christian name and where he lived; there had been that faint tremor of his expression at the mention of the date, there had been his strange silence about the identity parade—it did not add up to much for an evening's work, but it was something, and Terence salved his pride by telling himself that it was as much as anyone without official status could have found out. Without any permit, as it were, to ask questions and demand answers, the going was hard indeed.

When Terence let himself into his flat the telephone was ringing. He looked at his watch as he picked up the receiver. Half past eleven, yet it was Sylvia.

"I thought you said you'd ring," she began as soon as he put the phone to his ear. She sounded both aggressive and tearful.

Terence had to make a conscious effort to respond acceptably. Sylvia's complaints, indeed Sylvia herself, seemed completely irrelevant, but he apologized for not calling, then asked rather nervously where Edgar was.

"It's all right, he's having a shower," said Sylvia. "*Why* couldn't you ring?"

"I haven't been anywhere near a phone. If you want to know, I've been driving all over town."

"Driving?"

"In one of the firm cars," he improvised. "I had to hunt up some people who owe money."

"On Saturday night?"

He could tell she did not believe him. He could hardly blame her. "I had to catch them at home," he said. "Never mind about all that. Is there any chance of seeing you before Monday?"

"Before Tuesday you mean," she said. "I've already told you I have to go to the girls' school on Monday night. They're having a parents' evening."

He could tell from her tone that he should have remembered this. "Can't you skip the parents' evening?" he coaxed, hoping to flatter her with his ardor. "They wouldn't miss one mum among the hordes, and think what a lovely alibi you'd have for our rendezvous."

"Don't be silly, I have to go. It's a meet-the-teacher evening; I couldn't miss that."

"No, I don't suppose you could," he said, placating her. He felt quite unable to bear a quarrel with Sylvia on top of everything else. "Tuesday then. You'll come around, won't you?"

"If you want me to."

What was all this? "Of course I want you to. I only wish you could come round every night of the week."

"Me or some other woman?" Sylvia asked.

"Darling Sylvia, how ungrammatical," he said, playing for

71

time, wishing Edgar would emerge from the blasted bathroom and put an end to this tedious conversation. "What do you mean?"

"As long as you have some woman to go to bed with when you feel like it, it doesn't much matter to you who it is, does it?"

"Darling, how can you say such a thing?" asked Terence, putting as much reproach as possible into his voice. Actually he did think it a bit much for Sylvia to take that line, considering all the time and attention he had lavished on her in recent months. "You really know, don't you, that there's nobody else? I've told you often enough how I feel about you."

"You mean you love me? Why not say so straight out, then?"

"I have!"

"Then prove it by telling me what you were really up to this evening!"

"I *have* told you! Rounding up debtors for the firm."

Sylvia gave a disbelieving snort. Terence felt as indignant as if he had been telling the truth. Damn the woman! Why didn't she believe him? It was a perfectly plausible story. Fortunately at this point Sylvia apparently heard Edgar emerging from the bathroom, and she cut the conversation short by promising, or threatening, to come around on Tuesday about eight o'clock.

As she hung up, the first thought that came to Terence was that he had two clear days and nights before Tuesday, during which time he could pursue Chris Henderson without interference from Sylvia. He was a bit shaken when he realized what he was thinking. He had not known until then that he intended to do anything further about Henderson, but now he was seized by a tremendous impatience and felt he could hardly bear not knowing what Chris Henderson was up to at that moment.

He hurried out straight after a scratch breakfast in the morning, armed with his street directory and all the transport guides. Jellicoe Road, where the Hendersons lived, was just off a bus route; Terence reckoned he could get there with only three changes and a minimum of walking. It was Sunday morning, though, fairly early Sunday morning at that, the trains were running at long intervals, buses were few and far between, and there were no taxis roaming the suburban wastes. It therefore took Terence an hour and a half to get to Jellicoe Road. The place was rather more animated than when he had last seen it on the previous evening. People were out buying papers, walking dogs, pushing prams. The Hendersons' house looked the same, however, no morning face there. The curtains were still drawn, the door tight shut against the street. Terence lingered for a few minutes on the pavement outside, then went to the news agent on the corner and got an *Observer*. He wondered whether to mention the Hendersons to the old girl behind the counter, then decided against it. The shop was too close to the house; word would get back that inquiries were being made.

Using the paper as a shield and with his cap pulled low, he went back up the street and past the house. He risked a sideways glance—curtains still drawn, late risers apparently, but perhaps they were all sitting drinking tea in the kitchen out the back, father, mother and Chris. Terence wondered if there were any others in the family. He could not picture anyone else. Even the parents were shadowy. All his attention was focused on the boy. Meanwhile, what was he to do while he was waiting? There were no benches to sit on, it was not that kind of street, but he would not be conspicuous if he just stood still and waited. A number of people up and down the length of the street were doing just that, waiting for their dogs, waiting for the pubs to open, just waiting for something to happen. Terence took up his own position a little beyond where he had been parked the previous evening, near enough to see anyone leaving the house, too far away to be easily recognized.

He unfurled the paper and read it in snatches. Half an hour went slowly by, then everything happened at once. The Hendersons' door opened, Chris Henderson came running down the steps and was into his car and away round the corner and out of sight before Terence had wakened up to the fact that his quarry had come and gone and that there was absolutely nothing he could do about it. No cruising taxis, no bikes to be commandeered, no authority to shout "Stop that man!" He just had to let him go.

At least, however, he could now stroll about openly, without any danger of being recognized. Chris Henderson's father knew him slightly, of course, but even if he did notice him, which was hardly likely, it would not matter. Terence was sure Chris would not have mentioned their encounter at the garage. That narrow face was a secretive one, not given to gossip about the day's activities. So, shaking off his disappointment, Terence stepped out more boldly and confidently and stared at the Henderson's house brazenly as he passed it—nothing to see but at least he had given it a thorough inspection. He went on round a corner and came to a school, almost certainly the one the young Chris Henderson would have gone to. Infants one gate, Juniors the other, spikes on top of the brick wall and wire netting over the windows. Terence made a note of the name of the school, the name of the headmistress, and for good measure the name of the caretaker. It would after all be less than ten years since Chris Henderson had left this school. Someone there would possibly remember him.

On round another corner, and Terence checked the time on his watch. The pubs would be open; a pint at the local was called for. A quick survey showed there were two pubs within easy walking distance, The White Swan and The Feathers. He decided to try The Feathers first, because it was smaller and cozier, and for once that weekend he was lucky. He had hardly taken his first swallow when the door opened and the older Henderson came in. He was expected; two men made room for him at their table and had a drink waiting for him.

Terence, watching the three of them, drank some more of his beer, then decided on a bold approach. Glass in hand, he went over. "It's Mr. Henderson, isn't it?" he said.

One of the other men was telling a slow, involved story. He broke it off, and all three of them turned and looked up at Terence. They were not friendly but he managed to keep his cheery smile in place.

Henderson lowered his glass to the table. "That's me," he said with deliberation.

"It's you that's got the garage up the High Street, isn't it?"

"That's right."

"I used to bring my car in to you."

"That's right, you did. Mr. Lambert, isn't it?"

"You remember me, then," said Terence, enormously relieved. Surely things would go more easily now!

"You had an 1100. Green, wasn't it?"

"Yes. Dark green."

There was a pause. "You stopping round here, then?" Henderson asked reluctantly.

"Just passing through." Terence waited stolidly beside them, but no one said anything and he was forced to speak again. "Mind if I join you for a bit?" he asked with assumed brashness. The men shuffled a few inches along the seat and Terence squeezed into the small space they had made available. "Never cared much for drinking alone," he said, and found he was sweating. A detective, spy, inquiry agent clearly needed a thick skin.

The three men, having made room for him, now ignored him. The one who had been telling the story took it up again. They heard it through to the end, then went on to talk about the previous day's football, some local demolition project, a recent darts match. Terence sat stubbornly on, contributing an occasional safe remark, trying not to show any impatience, but time was passing and finally he leaned forward and broke clumsily in on their conversation.

"I was speaking to your boy the other day," he said directly to Henderson.

The three men fell silent and looked at Terence. "Oh, aye?" said Henderson.

"Up at the garage."

Henderson merely grunted, but one of the others said. "Up at the garage? That'll be Chris."

"Have you another boy, then?" asked Terence, again speaking directly to Henderson, seizing the opportunity of finding out more about the family.

Henderson shook his head definitely, almost contemptuously, still without speaking.

"You've got the girl, though," said the helpful friend.

"A married daughter, isn't it?" said Terence, forcing the pace.

Henderson took the cigarette out of his mouth and looked at Terence. "Aye, she's married," he said, and put the cigarette back between his lips with great deliberation.

Terence wanted to push on, to learn all he could about this family that was beginning to obsess him—"obsess" was the word he used to himself; it was an acknowledgment of his state of mind—but he recognized the signs. He knew he could go no further without antagonizing Henderson, so he bought a round of drinks and sat back, saying nothing more but determined to outwait his man. The doors now stayed shut against the sunny midday, people had stopped arriving, the pub was full. Terence, forced to be silent and apart, was disagreeably conscious of the noise, the smoke, the crowding, the smell of beer. But soon it was the turn of the tide; in ones and twos the customers drank up their last pints and went home to Sunday dinner. One of the three men went, then Henderson got heavily to his feet and lumbered off with the barest of nods, and Terence was left alone with the third man, the one who had earlier volunteered the information about the Henderson family. Terence's gamble had paid off. He bought the man another beer and hitched his chair closer.

"Been coming in here long?" he asked.

"Close on thirty years."

"As long as that?" said Terence, really surprised. Christ, he'd forgotten the lives some people lived. "What about the other two who were here? Have they been coming as long?"

"Henderson and them? Well, I been coming the longest, but Tom Henderson, he's been coming near as long. The other chap's new to here, you might say."

Terence took this to mean he had been coming in for only ten years or so but he was careful not to follow this up. He wanted to keep his companion on the right track. "You and Henderson must know each other pretty well by now, then."

"Well enough."

"Do you know Chris?"

"Henderson's boy?"

"That's right, Chris Henderson. Up at the garage." God give him patience! "How long has he been up there, do you know?"

"Up at the garage? Let's see now, he started there when he left school, and he left school the same time as our Willy. That'd make it six years, near enough."

"How old is he, then?"

"Chris? Twenty, twenty-one."

A couple of years older than Terence would have thought. "Not married, is he?"

"Married? No."

"Going steady?"

"Not that I know of."

"Some of these young chaps aren't much interested in girls," said Terence, hoping for something significant, but the response when it came was disappointingly general.

"Reckon some are more interested in football," said the other vaguely. "Or the dogs," he added as an afterthought.

"Do you mean Chris Henderson is?"

"Not that I know of. Nothing special." He began to button his coat, adjust his scarf.

Terence was baffled. He had found out very little. Perhaps his whole approach had been wrong. Perhaps right at the beginning he should have come out into the open and offered the old codger a pound or two for all he knew about the Hendersons. It was too late to do that even if it had been a good idea, because while he was hesitating the old man had got to his feet, nodded good-bye and shuffled away. Almost immediately the barmaid called, "Time!" and the pub slowly emptied.

Out on the pavement Terence was still reluctant to leave the district. He walked aimlessly round the shabby deserted streets, coming at last on a Greek restaurant, strange outpost of the Mediterranean. He pushed the door open hesitantly. The place was huge, cavernous and gloomy, empty except for two solitary men, swarthy and old, sitting at separate tables but reading copies of the same Greek newspaper. Terence, with a perception unusual for him, thought that this might very well be their weekly treat, a little leisure, a Greek meal, a paper from home. This glimpse of the essential cheerlessness of their lives depressed Terence; he deliberately sat where he could no longer see the two sad men. It was as though his own worries and perplexities were making him more aware of the cares of others. From the long, badly written menu he ordered taramasalata and kabobs, having pleasant holiday memories of these dishes, but the food when it came was not good. Terence was absurdly disappointed; he told himself childishly that nothing was going right.

He pushed his plate away and lit a cigarette and remembered that not far away was a famous house he had always intended visiting sometime. He asked the waiter for directions, but the waiter, elderly and forlorn like his regular customers, could not at first help him. Ah, but wait! In the local station there was a poster advertising just such a place. Perhaps he could go and see? Terence tipped him for his information and hurried off, as purposeful as if sightseeing was the main business of the afternoon. The notice at the station told him where to go. After a short walk he came to the beautiful building, gleaming white through the leafless trees, drifts of mauve and yellow crocuses the only color in a monochrome world.

The house, however, was still keeping winter hours and closed at four o'clock and Terence walked back through the gathering dusk to Jellicoe Road. This time it was completely deserted; the morning loiterers had all gone and no others had taken their places. The pubs of course were shut and so by now was the corner shop. Chris Henderson's car was not there but Terence realized it was just not possible to wait until it came back. It was cold, it was growing dark, Terence was conspicuous in the empty street and there was nowhere he could watch from and yet be out of sight. He gave up and went home.

He was annoyed with himself for giving up, however, dissatisfied with his whole day, disappointed with the little he had learned. He spent a wakeful night, and sometime in the early morning he decided that he would spend the whole of that day shadowing Chris Henderson.

He left the flat very early so as to be already at the garage when Henderson arrived; without a car it was not possible to pick up the trail at Henderson's house. This did not unduly worry him until he was actually traveling toward the High Street on the Underground, and then he suddenly wondered what he would do if Chris failed to show up. For the first time it occurred to him that on the previous day when Chris had shot off in his car and he had lost him, he might quite simply have been going to work—the garage was after all open on Sunday. Chris Henderson had certainly been at work on Saturday. If he had worked on Sunday as well it was very likely he would have Monday off. This line of thought made Terence extremely nervous and depressed. It was quite illogical, but he had by now so deeply involved himself in the whole business that he was quite incapable of shrugging off such a setback as just one of those things. He waited in an absolute fever of impatience for Henderson to arrive and when he did drive up soon after eight Terence felt quite weak with relief. He watched until Henderson was safely inside and waited a little longer until he glimpsed him in his mechanic's overalls, then judged it was safe to go down the street and ring the office from the call box there; it had been too early to phone before he left home. He had planned to tell them some small lie to explain his absence but in the act of dialing he suddenly rebelled at behaving like an office boy playing truant. When someone answered he merely said curtly he would not be in that day, and hung up.

That was at nine-fifteen. About twelve hours later, he decided to call it a day and go home to bed. The amount of information collected in that long stretch of time was quite literally nil. Henderson had worked all day at the garage, not even emerging at lunchtime. One of the boys had gone to a local café and bought a pile of sandwiches, pies and cakes which the mechanics had apparently eaten at work. At six o'clock Chris and his father had come out together, got into Chris's car and left with Chris driving. Terence, having had all day to think about what he would do when this happened, turned and ran along the street to catch the bus that would take him close to Jellicoe Road. When he got there, the car was parked at the curb and the Hendersons' curtains were tightly drawn. After that, for more than two hours, absolutely nothing happened, a total blank. Terence went home.

Earlier that day, between twelve and one, when Terence was eating a pie out of a paper bag, Sylvia was alone in her sunny kitchen having lunch—two rye biscuits, a tomato, a hard-boiled egg, a glass of Russian tea (unsweetened, of course). Sylvia was always dieting, or about to diet, or just coming off a diet. This was because although she herself was still slim and shapely, she had the awful example of her mother before her. Sylvia's mother had been slender, even thin, all through Sylvia's childhood, but then, inexplicably, in her early forties, she had suddenly put on a great deal of weight, and Sylvia, after having been used to the idea of a slim mother, had had to adjust to having a fat one instead. Sylvia's mother made no comparable adjustment; she made no concessions to her changed appearance at all, continuing to dress in the same styles and to eat the same foods, and Sylvia could only conclude that her mother's habits had become so set by middle age that she could not change them. To herself, Sylvia's mother was still the skinny little girl who had been encouraged to drink cream instead of milk, in order to fatten her up.

Sylvia was determined not to be trapped in the same way, so she dieted before she had to, and dressed with a rather severe elegance while she was still young enough to get away with more extreme fashions. Edgar approved of her taste in clothes as being ladylike and suitable. Terence also approved. He liked the contrast between the way she dressed and the way she behaved in private with him. He liked to look at her, so cool and poised, and to hug to himself his secret knowledge of her abandonment in love. Also, he liked the aura of money given off by her discreet chic.

Sylvia applied the same fastidious taste to the food she prepared. On this particular day, for instance, the tomato and egg were arranged on a Spode salad plate, the glass of Russian tea was in a silver holder, and it was all neatly set out on an embroidered cloth, with a matching napkin to hand.

Even so, Sylvia was not enjoying her lunch, and after only a few mouthfuls she pushed the rest aside and gave herself up to brooding. She was forced to admit to herself that she was jealous, and this hurt her pride. Always before, which meant before her marriage, it had been the other person who had been jealous, and Sylvia had been able to view his unhappiness and his absurd undignified behavior with detachment. Now she was the one who was unhappy and she felt in her bones that she was capable of acting ridiculously at any given moment. This realization, that neither her emotions nor her actions were any longer properly under control, frightened her. It was as though a comforting haze had been swept away and she saw a strange forbidding landscape at her very feet. Also, just when for the first time in her whole life she felt forlorn and unsure of herself, she had absolutely no one to turn to, seeing that Terence, who should have been her comfort, was the source of her misery. Their last conversation, which she had gone over and over in her mind, had been brief, hurried and most unsatisfactory. It was true they had arranged to meet on Tuesday evening, but that was still more than thirty hours away and Sylvia suddenly made up her mind that she was not going to wait docilely for all that time. She stood up abruptly and did something she had never done before. She rang Terence at his office.

He was not there. The voice at the other end said that he had called to say he would not be in at all that day. The person speaking sounded offended. Sylvia wondered briefly who had done the offending, Terence by ringing earlier, or herself by ringing now. She hung up and stood wondering what to do. One thing was sure, she could not just give up and do nothing. She wanted action, and in less than a minute she had made up her mind to go over to Terence's flat right away. Rapidly she tidied the kitchen and changed her clothes, but just as she was letting herself out of the house the telephone rang. She ran back inside and snatched up the receiver, but it was Edgar. She did not quite manage to keep the disappointment out of her voice, but Edgar apparently noticed nothing.

"I thought I had better remind you about tomorrow night," he said in explanation, "in case you'd forgotten."

"Forgotten what?"

"That we're going to dinner at the Frobishers'."

"Oh, my God!" said Sylvia.

"You had forgotten, then?"

"Absolutely."

"I suppose I should have reminded you earlier."

"No, it's not your fault, I've got it written down here. I should have checked to see what we've got on this week." Already Sylvia's mind was actively considering how this for-gotten engagement could be turned to advantage. At least the fact that she could not spend Tuesday evening at the flat as arranged gave her a sound excuse for going over there now. She did not stop to analyze why she felt she needed an excuse, but she got rid of Edgar on the phone rather brusquely and set out immediately for Terence's flat.

When she stepped off the bus near the flat it was still only half past one. If Terence were at home they could spend the whole afternoon together. The prospect excited her, and she was extremely disappointed when there was no reply to her knocking. She listened through the door, but there was no sound or movement discernible. She knocked again, even more loudly, and then reluctantly fumbled in her bag for the key which Terence had given her months ago and which she had never before had occasion to use. As she was unlocking the door she felt guilty and also just a little bit devalued— letting herself into the empty flat, she could no longer see herself as the pretty lady just visiting. In her own eyes her furtive behavior reduced her to an adulterous and infatuated woman, and she prowled around her lover's apartment like a spy. There was little there to notice, hardly anything she had never seen before, except that she was disconcerted to find how shabby and ordinary everything looked in the light of a winter's afternoon. She could not remember having seen the flat by daylight before and she realized for the first time how much it had owed its atmosphere to drawn curtains, shaded lamps and the phonograph turned down low—all the hackneyed attributes of a love nest. Now dust could be seen lying thick on every surface, the bed was unmade, the break- fast dishes still on the table, clothes had been tossed over the chairs and thrown on the floor, the afternoon view from the window was drab, even bleak. Sylvia longed to tidy every- thing, to wash the dishes and make the bed, to polish and dust, to switch on the heater and the lamps and banish the wintry gloom, but she held herself back. With her new caution, she was afraid of appearing possessive, and all she did was to clear a space on the sofa where she sat and waited, tense as a coiled spring. After half an hour she got up and made herself a cup of coffee. After another half hour she turned on the television and pretended to watch. Her eyes followed the flickering shadows but she heard nothing of what was being said, her ears being strained to catch the sound of Terence's arrival.

But he did not come. She could not stay later than five o'clock; even that was really too late and would involve her in lying explanations to the girls. She took her cup and saucer out to the kitchen to wash them and while she was standing at the sink a little white cat jumped onto the sill outside the window and meowed confidently to be let in. Sylvia looked through the glass at the pretty cat and wondered how often it came. It was very tame; it might even belong to Terence, but he had never mentioned it. Sylvia saw it as a symbol of the part of Terence's life which was hidden from her, and she drew the curtains sharply together against its intrusion. After all, she told herself, it was getting dark.

Back in the living room she found a pencil and a piece of paper and wrote a note saying she would ring him later that evening, but when she thought about it she realized she was sick and tired of telephone conversations. It was days since she had seen him; on an impulse she tore up the note and scribbled another saying that she would come around that night after the school meeting. This was madness, and she knew it, but she left the message propped up on the table and went away without changing her mind.

Edgar was disposed to go with Sylvia that evening to the parents' meeting at the school but she quickly discouraged him, saying that there was no need for the two of them to go out on a cold night to what was really only a routine function as far as they were concerned. "After all, darling," she said, "it's not as though we're worried about the girls in any way. We've got no problems to talk over with the teachers."

Edgar allowed himself to be persuaded to stay at home, but he delayed his decision until the last possible minute, so Sylvia had no time to relax before dashing off to the school. She sat tensely through the principal's opening remarks and was first on her feet when those present were asked to make their way to their daughters' classrooms. She went to see Marion's teacher first and was able to be at the head of the queue of parents there. The interview was satisfactory too, brisk and to the point. Marion was working well, she had a good attitude to things, she was taking part in all class activities, she could perhaps devote a little more attention to presentation—her work was not always as neat as was desirable, but that of course was a relatively minor matter. Otherwise everything was fine. Sylvia, suitably gratified, thanked the teacher and made her way quickly along the corridors to Julie's room. There was a long line of parents ahead of her there, and she awaited her turn impatiently, staring at each of the ones being interviewed in turn, willing them to stand up and go away, grudging them every minute of their conversation with Julie's teacher. When at last it was Sylvia's turn it was already a quarter to ten. As she sat down she was calculating: twenty minutes at least to get to the flat, half an hour to get back from there to the house, half past eleven was the latest possible time she could get home with the school meeting as her sole alibi, that gave her less than an hour with

Terence, without counting the time she would have to spend talking to Julie's teacher. She wished frantically she had not stopped to see her, but even as she wished it she knew that she could not have avoided it, as she could neither have admitted to Julie that she had not spoken to her teacher, nor lied to her that she had. She was determined, however, not to talk for long. Miss Clifton, though, was apparently not in a hurry.

"Ah, Mrs. Manson," she greeted her, "I'm pleased you were able to come along." Sylvia smiled and waited, resisting the temptation to sneak a look at her watch. "Of course, we are always glad to see any parents at any time," Miss Clifton went on. "There's no need to wait until one of these special evenings if there is anything really worrying you." Here she paused and shuffled the papers in front of her, and Sylvia risked a glance at her watch. Ten to. Miss Clifton found the sheet of paper she was apparently looking for and placed it on top of the pile. Then she looked across at Sylvia again. "We thought you might be getting in touch with us before now, Mrs. Manson," she said.

With difficulty, Sylvia brought her thoughts back from Terence and tried to attend to what was being said. "What do you mean?" she asked uncertainly. "Why would I be getting in touch with you?"

Her blank incomprehension embarrassed Miss Clifton. The school teacher fiddled with her pencil and tried again. "All of us here have noticed such a change in Julie over the last few weeks," she said. "Julie has always been such a good girl up till now."

Dear God, what was all this? Sylvia knew she should concentrate, but she could not forget how the minutes were ticking away. "Do you mean she's not a good girl any longer?" she asked.

But Miss Clifton shied away from this bluntness. "Oh, I wouldn't say that exactly," she said. "After all, a great many girls go through these difficult phases and get over them completely, and we are sure that Julie will too, eventually. But I'm afraid that at the moment she is being difficult. In fact, Mrs. Manson, we have put her on a weekly report."

"A weekly report!" exclaimed Sylvia, and glanced around to see if anyone had overheard, but the teacher's desk was isolated on a platform and the remaining parents were talking among themselves. She turned back to Miss Clifton. "Surely that wasn't necessary," she said coldly.

"I'm sorry, Mrs. Manson, but I'm afraid we thought it was."

"But Julie's never given the slightest trouble, she's always had good reports, she's always been so happy at school, not only this school but every school she's been at."

"We know that, Mrs. Manson, and believe me we are all most concerned at the change in her."

"Why didn't you get in touch with us?"

"If I hadn't seen you tonight I would have considered it my duty to write to you, but frankly, Mrs. Manson, as I said earlier, we have been expecting *you* to contact *us.*"

"Why would we?" cried Sylvia. "How could we know there was anything wrong?"

"Well, for one thing, Julie has done virtually none of the homework set for the past month. Surely you must have noticed she hasn't been working? With A levels coming up in a few weeks' time?"

"Julie goes to her room every evening," said Sylvia. "Naturally her father and I assumed she was working."

"I'm afraid not," said Miss Clifton. "Also, it has come to light just this afternoon that she played truant on two occasions recently."

"When?"

Miss Clifton referred to the paper in front of her. "She was absent from school for the last two periods of Thursday last week, and for the whole afternoon of the previous Tuesday."

"And you have only just found out?" said Sylvia accusingly.

"It is our policy to give the sixth form a fair amount of independence," said Miss Clifton frostily. "They are not under such strict supervision as the rest of the school."

"I am very sorry to hear all this," said Sylvia, equally coldly, drawing on her gloves as she spoke. "Her father and I shall speak to Julie in the morning."

She made to get up, but Miss Clifton held up her hand to delay her. "I'm afraid there is more," she said. "I have here a summary of Julie's weekly reports."

But Sylvia ignored the implied request to remain seated. She stood up and said firmly, "I hardly think this is the time and place to discuss this business in detail, Miss Clifton. After we have spoken to Julie I shall ring and make an appointment to see Miss Webster." Miss Webster was the principal.

Miss Clifton also stood up. "I was hoping to explain about the weekly reports," she began, but Sylvia cut in.

"I truly think that it would be best to postpone all that," she said crisply.

"As you wish," said Miss Clifton. "Good evening, Mrs. Manson." She sat down abruptly and nodded to the next hovering parent.

By the time Sylvia reached the front door of the school she was almost running. It was a quarter past ten. "You're in a hurry to get home!" someone who knew her called out. She smiled mechanically at him and slowed down until he was out of sight, then hurried again.

Once in a taxi she found she was shaking. What was all this business about Julie? She knew she had handled things badly. She had snubbed and antagonized Miss Clifton, she had failed to show sufficient concern or appreciation of the gravity of the matter. She should have stayed for as long as Miss Clifton wanted her to, she should have found out as much as she could, she should have gone home and talked it over with Edgar straightaway, yet here she was instead, hurrying to a mad, clandestine meeting with her lover. She was ashamed of herself but she did not for one moment consider leaning forward and asking the driver to take her home instead. Her whole being was set on seeing Terence as soon as possible even if only for less than half an hour.

Yet when Terence opened the door to her, she immediately began telling him about the trouble with Julie. He was disconcerted. He had read her note with mixed feelings. Of course he would be glad to see her, very glad—she was still his darling love—but he was uneasily conscious of how indiscreet this meeting was, so hurried, so late at night, and besides, he had been counting on having until the following evening to decide how much he could tell Sylvia about his recent activities and the necessity of making an earlier decision flustered him. He had come to precarious terms with all this, and now Sylvia had thrown him by all this obscure talk about weekly reports and playing truant. He listened sympathetically at first because it was Sylvia who was worried, but in the end he became impatient.

"Never mind all that now," he said. "We've got only a few

minutes. Let's not spend the whole time wondering what sort of mess Julie's got herself into."

"There's no need to speak in that heartless way," said Sylvia. "Even though you don't know Julie she *is* my daughter and I thought you'd care about her being in trouble."

Terence put his arm about her. "I do care, darling," he said, patting her soothingly, "and I'm very sorry about it all, but you can't blame me for wanting you to think a little bit about me too. After all, you've got hours to devote to Julie and the others and only a few miserable minutes for me."

Sylvia pushed his arm away and sat up straight. "That's nonsense," she said. "You obviously don't understand at all. The trouble with you, Terence, is that you're jealous. You resent the girls."

"You certainly seem more involved with them than you are with me," he said. Even as he spoke he knew he was being absurd.

Sure enough, Sylvia looked extremely exasperated at this remark. "It's all very well for you," she began, "with nobody but yourself to think about."

"I think about you," he said, but she ignored him and swept on to outline in passionate detail the difference between his carefree bachelor existence and her committed life. "You can just take a day off whenever you feel like it," she cried. "Like today. Where were you anyhow? At the races? Gadding about town?"

"Would you like to know where I was?" he demanded, stung. "If you want to know, I was tailing your damned red-headed murderer, that's what I was doing."

Sylvia was immediately subdued. She stared at him, her eyes dilating. "What?" she said, in little more than a whisper. "What did you say you were doing?"

Terence was already regretting having been provoked into saying so much. "Nothing really," he said, very offhand. "It's just that I saw a chap who looked like your description of that man, so I followed him for a bit."

"But I don't understand!" she said. "You mean you saw a red-haired man, so you followed him in case he was the one I saw?"

"It wasn't quite like that," he said, ill at ease. "I saw a man acting in a funny way—he was sort of sneaking along, and the way he moved reminded me of what you said about that chap, and then I noticed he had red hair as well so I thought it was worth trying to find out what he was up to."

"When was this?"

"When? Oh, this morning."

"What time?"

"Christ, I don't know. Eleven o'clock, maybe."

"So that wasn't why you didn't go to work?"

"No, of course it wasn't. I didn't go to work because I didn't feel like it. Satisfied?"

"No, I'm not," said Sylvia. "It all seems pretty funny to me. How long did you say you were following this man?"

"All day. Ever since about eleven o'clock, that is."

"You're mad," said Sylvia. "I don't suppose you found out anything. Did you?"

"Not much."

"I bet you didn't."

"What's the matter?" he cried. "Don't you believe me?"

"No," she said. "And if I did believe you I'd think you were stark staring mad. Why did you have to bring this up again, just when I'd almost managed to forget all about it?"

Terence felt a sulky resentment against her. "Well, I haven't forgotten," he retorted. "I thought you were so bloody sorry for all those poor girls, as you called them, and now you've put it all right out of your mind and that means you want me to put it out of my mind too. They haven't caught that chap yet, you know."

"And I suppose you're going to spend all tomorrow hunting for him too, are you?" she said, with sarcasm.

"I might," he said.

She stared at him, frowning, forced to take him seriously. "I really believe you might," she said slowly. "Terence, promise me you won't do anything so absolutely crazy. Go on, promise me," she repeated urgently as he stayed silent.

"Why don't you want me to?" he asked.

She made an impatient gesture, flinging up her hands, then noticed the time. "I must go, I must go," she exclaimed in panic, gazing wildly around for her handbag, her coat, her gloves. "It's after eleven, I must go, don't stop me."

He followed her to the door, went with her to get a taxi. One came, and as he put her into it he saw she was on the verge of tears. She looked distraught, her face above the fur collar was white and strained. He felt a cold weight settle on him. What would be the end of it all? They had been right in the beginning to shut the world out. Now they had allowed the wall they had built around them to be breached and he had this dark feeling that they were about to be engulfed in troubles. He longed passionately to withdraw, to retreat. Watching the taxi bearing Sylvia weeping away from him, Terence swore to himself he would have nothing further to do with the sinister boy from the garage.

This resolution carried him through the rest of the evening, and allowed him to go to sleep that night. It was as though his decision was a talisman, a charm against any further catastrophe, and in the morning he superstitiously avoided even thinking about the Hendersons, father and son. He went extra early to the office and immersed himself in the pile of work which had accumulated on his desk.

When Sylvia arrived home, she found Edgar still up, waiting for her, and she immediately used the trouble about Julie as her excuse for coming home so late. She implied that Miss Clifton had asked her to stay behind so that they could discuss Julie's recent conduct, and driven into a corner by Edgar's questions she had actually declared that as a result of their long talk she had missed the last bus home and had had to wait for ages for a taxi. Even as she was saying this she knew it was a very risky lie and she tried to bury it straightaway in an involved and incoherent recital of Julie's misdemeanors.

Edgar's first, startled reaction had been to lose his temper with her. "You should have taken the car!" he cried. "I keep on telling you to take the car. Instead you have all this ridiculous traipsing about the streets, spending hours waiting about for buses and taxis. You're mad!"

"It's the night driving!" she cried.

"A ridiculous affectation," he shouted. He swung around and glared at the clock. "It's after midnight," he said. "After midnight! The circular said the meeting would be over by ten."

"They always say that," said Sylvia, "and they never are. Anyhow, haven't you been listening? It's *Julie* we should be talking about. Not me, Julie."

"Yes," he said, in a much quieter voice. "Julie. What's this all about, then?"

"I don't know," said Sylvia, gesturing hopelessly. "It's what

I've just told you. She's not working, she's making no attempt to work, she's being difficult, rude and sulky with everyone, some days she hasn't even been going to school. She's been playing *truant*, Edgar. Julie, playing truant!"

Edgar looked suddenly old and tired, and Sylvia, watching him, felt fiercely angry with Julie for upsetting Edgar and disrupting their family life, but at the same time she was wretchedly miserable because things had apparently gone so wrong for the child.

"I can't believe it, you know," Edgar said in a subdued and anxious way. "I simply can't believe that Julie would behave like that."

"I couldn't believe it either, at first," said Sylvia, in just as muted a voice. "But I'm very much afraid it's true."

They talked for a long time after that, well into the early hours, and in the morning they spoke to Julie, cornering her in the dining room when she came down to practice the piano before breakfast. She broke away from them, though, and ran upstairs and slammed the door and refused to answer them when they called to her. This behavior made it clear to them that what Sylvia had been told at school was indeed true. Julie had turned against the school and now she was evidently rejecting them as well. Marion emerged scared and sleepy from her room, and her father, balked in his attempt to communicate with Julie, turned on her instead, and cross-examined her until she burst into tears and admitted that quite often—"Quite often!" exclaimed Sylvia—Julie had not gone to school at all. She said that Julie had made her promise not to tell anybody about this, and she said over and over again that she had no idea where Julie went, Julie had never told her anything at all about it. Edgar was angrily skeptical, but Sylvia believed Marion, Julie having been revealed as being so secretive.

No one was hungry, but from habit Sylvia prepared breakfast, and the three of them sat down to it, but it was no good. They had never been a family for scenes and quarrels, they could not take this business in their stride and behave normally. The thought of Julie, hostile and in trouble, brooding in the room over their heads oppressed them almost unbearably and half a dozen times Sylvia made as if to go up to her, but she either restrained herself or was restrained by the others. They agreed that later, when Julie was calmer and more reasonable, they would try to discuss the whole matter with her. But while they were still sitting at the table pretending to eat they heard the front door close. They ran out into the hall but Julie was gone, down the road and out of sight before they got as far as the gate. Edgar took the car out and drove to the station, then around the neighboring streets, but Julie was nowhere to be seen. When he came back to the house Sylvia met him at the door and told him that Julie had left her school uniform in a heap on the bedroom floor and had apparently left wearing her orange trouser suit, but a frantic check showed that she had taken no extra clothes, no bag, nothing for the night, and as far as any of them knew she had virtually no money, so they clung to the thought that she meant to return that night.

The day was interminable, a nightmare. Edgar stayed home from the office, and Marion would have stayed home from school if they had let her, but by forcing themselves to speak sensibly and optimistically Sylvia and Edgar persuaded her to go. Once she was out of the house, however, they were unable to keep up this pretense of being calm. In fact they were swept with panic. Edgar got into the car again and spent two hours driving to every place he could think of where Julie could conceivably be, but of course he failed to find her—he was hopelessly out of touch with her activities. Sylvia stayed by the telephone. She was sitting by it there in the hall when Edgar went out; she was still there when he came back.

"I'm going to ring the police," she announced immediately on seeing him, but he replied wearily that she could not, Julie had not been gone long enough.

"They'd only laugh at you," he said, "when they hear she's been gone less than four hours."

"Even though she's only sixteen?"

"Sixteen? Sixteen's an adult these days. You've only got to read the papers."

"The papers are full of sixteen-year-old girls who get into trouble, if that's what you mean." But Sylvia had to admit there was sense in what Edgar said; there was not much point in ringing the police as yet, but she declared that if Julie was not home by nine o'clock that night nothing would stop her from reporting her absence. Twelve hours was quite long enough for her to be gone.

But in the end Julie walked in soon after six, not much later than if she had been to school. In reply to her parents' anxious questions she said shortly that she had gone to town.

"But you had no money!" said Sylvia.

"I walked."

"But what about food? What about lunch?"

"I wasn't hungry," Julie replied, but she did not look at her mother, and it occurred to Sylvia that the girl had probably hitchhiked to town and had possibly cadged a meal from the driver. Girls did that sort of thing, she knew, though in spite of everything she could hardly imagine her pretty, gentle Julie being so brazen. But at least she was now home and apparently intending to stay there; there was no talk about going away. Julie took her coat off and flung herself on the sofa in front of the television, snapped at Marion and ignored Edgar's reproofs, but clearly her mood had changed since the morning. Tense though Sylvia was, she realized the wise thing to do was to let the girl be. There was nothing to be gained and a great deal to be lost through forcing the pace.

In any case, there was no time to discuss anything at length if they were to go out for dinner as they had promised. Sylvia had been on the point of phoning the Frobishers to cancel the arrangement, when Julie had walked in; in a way, with Julie safely at home, this change of plan seemed unnecessary, not worth the social inconvenience, and besides, what excuse could they give for not going? Sylvia had not rung earlier; she had no intention of telling anyone at all about Julie's behavior and there were difficulties involved in inventing a sudden illness for any of them. It really seemed safer as well as simpler to go, and then when she and Julie were alone in the room for a moment Julie said something that made Sylvia decide very abruptly to get Edgar away from Julie and out of the house for the evening.

Looking across at her, Julie had said, "I wouldn't have thought you'd worry about a little thing like playing truant, Mother, considering."

"What do you mean by that?" Sylvia had asked sharply, too sharply for innocence, and Julie had answered, "You know very well what I mean. I'm not the only one in the family who's been doing something she shouldn't."

At that moment the door opened and Marion came in, followed by Edgar. Sylvia knew she should scotch this firmly, should boldly tackle Julie and force her to retract. Julie could not be as sure as she sounded; she was probably longing to be flatly contradicted, but with the others there Sylvia's nerve failed. Her one thought was to get Edgar out of the house, out of range, out of danger, until she could fix things with Julie, so she immediately turned to him and reminded him that it was time to be getting ready to go out.

Edgar was surprised and relieved. He felt they ought to go, but he had been expecting that Sylvia would be reluctant to leave the girls, and here she was positively urging him to hurry up and change. Certainly it was already nearly seven. The two of them dressed hastily, Sylvia interrupting her preparations several times to run downstairs to give some further warning or instruction to the girls, and then they drove across town to arrive in the end only a quarter of an hour or so past the time given.

The dinner party was a bore, as Sylvia at any rate had expected it would be. It was given by a middle-aged couple, pleasant enough, too much so to be successful hosts, as they included most of their acquaintances on their invitation list and conscientiously invited them in turn, letting duty rather than pleasure be their guide, so that all their parties foundered under the dead weight of dull but deserving guests. Sylvia was privately convinced that Edgar, and by association she herself, came into that category, and this belief inhibited her, cramped her style, so that at the Frobishers' she always *felt* a middle-aged, middle-class housewife and consequently kept on hearing herself talk like one. This evening, as usual, the conversation all seemed to be about schools and au pair girls and holidays on the Costa Brava. Sylvia could hardly bear it and as soon as she decently could she caught Edgar's eye and they made their excuses. It had been a tiring day, she said. Their kind hostess had no idea how tiring.

They were the first to leave; the party had barely finished their second cups of coffee. As they drove away, leaving the others still there, it was as though they were escaping. In spite of everything their spirits rose. They laughed together a little over the tedium of the evening, then Edgar switched on the car radio, in time to hear a news broadcast. The announcer told them calmly that another girl had been found murdered in a suburban street.

Sylvia turned fiercely on Edgar, beat on his left arm with her fist. "That could have been Julie!" she cried. "Do you realize, that could have been Julie!" and she broke into a storm of weeping.

Alone in his flat, Terence heard the same announcement. He had not been home long. After a busy, blameless day at the office, he had gone to the lift, intending to catch a bus from the stop near his office, but once in the lift he had abruptly, without conscious premeditation, pushed the button for the basement garage. It was exactly as though he were yielding to some overwhelming temptation. Even as he got the keys from the janitor, even as he took out a firm car, he knew that he was acting irrationally, that he was obsessed. He knew it, but it made no difference. Once again he drove to the garage, then to the house in Jellicoe Road, where he waited, sitting quietly in the parked car, from twenty-five past six until a quarter to eight. Then Chris Henderson had emerged, natty in sheepskin jacket and polished shoes, hair freshly brushed, and smoking a cigarette, and had driven away in a northerly direction. Terence had followed him, peering ahead along the badly lit streets, swearing at the red lights, accelerating on the straight empty roads, but then somewhere among the sleazy streets behind some public baths he had lost him. He had driven around the area for half an hour or more, but in the end had given it up as hopeless and driven back to the office, where he gave the night watchman five shillings to unlock the basement garage and put the car away. Then, tired, unable to face the long bus ride back to the flat, he had hailed a taxi and gone home.

He mixed himself a drink and listened to a jazz program on the radio. When it finished he intended to switch off and go to bed, but he sat on and listened idly to the late news. The third item was the murder of a girl not more than a quarter of a mile from where Terence had lost Chris. The announcer went on to link this with the attacks on other girls in the same district. Terence sat as if frozen, his drink halfway to his mouth, and then, coming to life, he put his glass down on the table and walked straight out of the flat, without his coat, leaving the light on and the radio still going. He went to the police station and gave information against Chris Henderson.

two

At the police station everything went as smoothly as if it had been rehearsed. Terence was almost sure it was the same constable on duty as when they had held the identification parade, and he came around in front of the desk and took Terence through to the back room as he had that other time. Terence was not at all surprised to find Inspector Quirke sitting there as though he were waiting for him. Somehow it all seemed inevitable, and the inspector listened to what Terence had to say with a calm attention that Terence found extremely soothing. It was as he imagined going to confession must be, and walking home afterward he felt relaxed, almost happy, as though a weight had been lifted off him.

Inspector Quirke called the sergeant in and said, "Lambert's prepared to swear to Henderson."

"What took him so long to come to the point?" asked the sergeant.

"He says it's because he found he knew the chap. Couldn't believe he'd do a thing like that."

"Do you think that's all there was to it, sir?"

"I don't know. I've had this feeling all along that there's something else there. But what brought him along tonight was the affair this evening. He says he saw Henderson only a couple of streets away, at about ten past nine."

The sergeant whistled. "Did he now!" he said.

Terence went out early the following morning and bought all the papers. Standing right there in the street he went hurriedly through them. They all reported the murder, giving it greater or less emphasis, but none of them mentioned Chris Henderson. Terence had not expected them to, could not logically have expected it, yet he felt let down, after the tension of the previous night.

When he got back to the flat the phone was ringing. It was Sylvia and as soon as Terence heard her he realized she was half hysterical. She immediately began to talk in a rapid, high-pitched voice about the murder and about Julie, something about Julie—she seemed to be making some sort of connection.

Terence, taken aback, tried to listen carefully, to find out what Julie had to do with it, but it was impossible to concentrate. He was uneasily conscious that it was not yet eight o'clock. Edgar and the girls must still be at home. Where was Sylvia calling from, for God's sake? If she was at home her voice must be carrying all over the house, and she was saying whatever came into her head, without bothering to wrap it up at all. Listening to her, thinking of the others listening to her, Terence began to sweat.

He managed to interrupt her at the third attempt. "Has anything actually happened to Julie?" he demanded.

"She hasn't been *murdered*, if that's what you mean."

"But she hasn't even been attacked, has she?"

"Even!"

Terence gripped the phone tightly. "Sylvia," he said slowly and carefully, "what is all this about Julie? What has happened?"

"She ran away," said Sylvia. "She was away all day yesterday, and we didn't know where she was."

"Where is she now?" asked Terence, and held his breath as he waited for Sylvia to reply.

"She's here," said Sylvia, and he let his breath out in a long sigh of relief.

"Thank God for that," he said. "Thank God she's safe."

"She's safe now," said Sylvia, "but she could have been murdered, just like this other poor girl. That man's a maniac, Terence. It's a nightmare; I should have gone to the police. If I had, this girl wouldn't have been killed. You should have *made* me go."

"How could I have made you?" Terence cried, but she ignored him and swept on.

"I've thought about it all night—I haven't slept at all—and I've made up my mind. I'm just ringing to tell you, I'm going to the police this morning to describe that man to them."

"There's no need for you to go," he said. "I've gone."

"Gone to the police?" she cried. "What do you mean? You went to the police weeks ago, and obviously your description wasn't good enough. I'll have to go myself and tell them exactly what I saw."

"Wait a minute," he said. "You don't understand; I went to the police again last night."

"What did you tell them?"

"I told them I saw that redheaded chap again, last night near where the girl was murdered."

"But how could you have? Do you mean to say you followed him again, after promising not to?"

"I didn't promise any such thing," he said angrily, "and it's a damned good thing I did follow him."

"You didn't stop him from killing that girl."

The rage died out of him. "No, I didn't," he said, "but I may have stopped him from killing anyone else."

"The police still have to find him," said Sylvia. "Always supposing the man you followed was the murderer. You didn't actually see him attacking the girl, did you, so how can you be sure?"

"For God's sake, Sylvia," he said tightly, "I didn't tell the police I was sure. I merely told them I saw Chris Henderson last night, and that I'd seen him attack that other girl back in January."

There was dead silence at the other end of the line, then Sylvia asked, "See who?" and he realized how much she still didn't know.

"Look here," he said hurriedly, "I haven't had time to tell you, but I found out his name. He's actually someone I know slightly."

"But even if you saw him last night, you didn't actually see him in January, did you?"

"No, but you did."

"But I don't know him," she pointed out, "so how do I know if it was him I saw or not? And anyhow, you've told the police that *you* saw him. What have you let us in for?"

"I haven't let you in for anything," he pointed out. Where the hell were her family?

"You might have," she said, her voice rising in panic again, "now that things have gone so far. And how do you know this person anyway? Why didn't you tell me you knew him? What's going on?"

Terence felt a strong urge to shake her, to shout at her, to bang the receiver down in her ear, but he controlled himself. "Look, Sylvia," he said urgently, "I'll explain everything to you when I see you. I promise. And as for going to the police, don't you see I had to? I had no choice. You felt the same way after all, and another thing, I went to the police in the first place because you wanted me to. In fact, you kept on and on at me until I did, remember?"

Sylvia began to cry. "So now I'm to blame if anything happens," she sobbed.

Terence felt helpless and apprehensive. "Don't, Sylvia," he said. "It'll be all right. Don't cry, someone will hear you."

"The door's shut."

She *was* calling from home then. "Look, Sylvia," he said again, "we'd better not talk any longer. Don't worry, there's a good girl; it'll be all right in the end, you'll see."

"I'll die if it all comes out," she said.

When Terence put the phone down he realized he was shaking with tension and frustration. To think it was *Sylvia* who had had this effect on him. Who would have thought she would go to pieces so easily? Always before she had been so gay, so dashing, almost reckless, in fact. Terence lit a cigarette and tried to work out how he felt about the whole situation. Logically, he should welcome anything that would force an open break between Sylvia and her husband, as this business might very well do unless Sylvia controlled herself better, but the whole issue had become so tangled. The two of them would really have to sort it all out the very next time they were together. But then with a jolt Terence realized they had rung off without making any arrangement to meet. That would have been unthinkable up till then.

Sylvia realized the same thing as soon as she had hung up, and in her low state of mind the omission took on a brooding significance. She found she just could not imagine the next step. Terence had sounded so irritable and impatient with her that she was miserably convinced he would not be wanting to see her again for a long time, if ever, and because of this she felt that she could never under any circumstances bring herself to call him. Sitting there in the cold bedroom she foresaw their affair petering out because neither of them could face speaking to the other. Time passed and she became uneasy about Edgar and the girls. She had stayed in bed pleading a sick headache, easily understandable in view of yesterday's anxiety, and she had asked to be left alone, but their prolonged silence suddenly seemed ominous to her. Supposing someone had been listening outside the door, or worse still, on the downstairs phone? She went cold at the thought, was rigid for an instant with horror, then was seized with a frantic desire to find out at all costs. She jumped out of bed and pulled on her dressing gown with feverish haste, shuffling her feet into slippers as she ran across the room. Heart racing, she jerked open the door. Nobody there, no one on the stairs, no one in the downstairs hall. The door to the dining room was closed. She opened it, and the three sitting at the table turned to look at her. Edgar got to his feet. Somehow this seemed terribly funny to Sylvia, along the lines of "The condemned man ate a hearty breakfast"—"The guilty wife was shown every courtesy"—and she had to crush down an insane impulse to giggle.

"Are you feeling a bit better?" Marion asked.

Sylvia nodded, confined herself to an apologetic smile, forced herself to take her usual seat at the table. "I felt like some coffee," she said, and watched while Edgar poured her a cup. Sipping it, she looked at each face in turn, Edgar's tired, Julie's wan (at least she was in her school uniform), Marion's fresh and rosy by comparison, and she had no idea what any of them was thinking, whether any of them knew what she had been doing. They were as inscrutable as red Indians. She had a sudden frightening sense of absolute isolation. Never before in her entire life had she had this feeling of being utterly on her own. She saw herself cut off from her family, abandoned by her lover.

Yet Terence rang her that very afternoon. In the intervening few hours he had forgotten or minimized his morning irritation in the face of an urgent and growing need to communicate. The pair of them were like collaborators in some crime who could speak openly only to each other. Besides, Terence had suddenly had the idea of taking Sylvia to see Chris Henderson, from a distance of course. As soon as this occurred to him, he cursed himself for not having thought of it earlier. At that moment it seemed to him that if only Sylvia would confirm that Henderson was the man she had seen from the window, all his worries would be over. Knowing that he was indeed the man, he would swear without a qualm to having seen him in the act, even though he had to do it in court and under oath. With Sylvia secretly but positively backing him, he would have no feelings of guilt if Chris Henderson was arrested, even convicted, on his evidence. His perjury in that case would be purely technical, able to be ignored and forgotten in the future. In a swelling access of hope he phoned Sylvia. He wanted her to come with him that same evening and to wait outside the garage to see Henderson leaving at about six. She declared, though, that she could not possibly come at that time, that it was the worst, the most inconvenient time he could have suggested, that he *knew* she could never, never get away in the late afternoon, and so on, but as he felt by now that he could not endure another night without her corroboration in the matter of the January attacker's identity, his determination wore her down, so that in the end she agreed to meet him at the bus stop nearest the garage at a quarter to six. When she hung up she had no idea what she would tell the family as an excuse, but it turned out to be quite simple. It happened to be the local late shopping night and when the girls came in at five she merely said she was going up the street to buy some odds and ends she had forgotten earlier, and walked out.

She took a taxi to the bus stop, then had to wait until Terence arrived by bus. He jumped off while it was still moving and hurried up to her, thinking she would need comfort and reassurance, but he found her looking quite composed and rather smarter even than usual, in a suit he had not seen her wear before. She greeted him coldly; evidently he was not to be forgiven just yet for his secrecy and his insistence on the meeting. As they walked away together, however, she unbent a little and remarked that he looked tired.

He seized on the opening. "I'm worried, Sylvia," he said. "You've got to admit I'm in a hell of a position. I hardly slept at all last night and I was afraid I wouldn't sleep tonight either unless you had a look at this chap. That's why I *had* to get you to come. I *had* to see you tonight. Was it all right, getting away?"

"I managed," she said. "Is that the garage over there?"

They took up their position opposite, half hidden by a phone booth, and within a few minutes the men started to leave. Terence knew most of them by sight now. He even fancied he was beginning to know them as people. He knew which ones went straight home, which ones regularly turned into the pub on the corner. One of them, a little fat one, had a car, a blue Prefect, in which he gave two of the others a lift every evening. Terence found himself wondering if they chipped in with the petrol, then jerked his thoughts back to the job in hand. He could not afford to let his attention wander—Chris Henderson could be across the pavement and into his car in a couple of seconds and all hope of Sylvia seeing him that evening would be lost. Terence fixed his eyes on the garage door and stared so unblinkingly at it that his whole body was stiff with tension, his stomach muscles tight and uncomfortable with nerves. Once, Sylvia started to speak but he hushed her fiercely. She felt him quivering beside her and, respecting his concentration, she stayed quiet and watched the door too.

Just when her eyes were beginning to water with the cold and the fixity of her attention, Terence gave her a great nudge. "There he is!" he said in a loud whisper. "There he is, just coming out."

"Where?" she asked anxiously, flustered by his excitement. "Which one?"

"There," he said. "There, just going over to the car, with the brown jacket."

A narrow, pale face, a glimpse of red hair, a general impression of restless youth, and he was gone. Sylvia stared after the car as it roared away down the street and could hardly believe the moment was over so quickly. "Well?" Terence said urgently. "What do you say?"

"I hardly know," she said. "He was gone so fast, I just got a glimpse of him."

"But was it the one?" he insisted. "Come *on*, Sylvia, you must know. It was, wasn't it?"

113

But she was slow, confused. "It's been so long, and then I only got this glimpse. I can't say for sure, Terence."

He felt an enormous disappointment and a surge of panic. "Come on, Sylvia, surely you can remember what he looked like," he pleaded. "Surely to God you can say whether this chap is him or not!"

His urgency made her stubborn. "It's no use, Terence, I can't swear to it," she said, reproving him.

"But I might have to!" he cried. "Do you realize I might have to swear to it literally, in court?"

"But that's perjury," she said, her hand to her mouth. "If you stand up in court and say you saw this man last January that'll be perjury, won't it?"

"Of course it will," he said, frowning at her in exasperation. "That's why I didn't want to say anything in the first place, remember?"

She stared at him, eyes dark with consternation in her pale face. "Oh, Terence," she said, "why did this have to happen?"

Later that evening at the police station Inspector Quirke said to the sergeant, "Anything to report about Henderson?"

"No, sir," said the sergeant. "Behaving quite normally, going to work and so forth. Stayed home last night. Only one thing—our man says Lambert was up at the garage last night, apparently keeping an eye on Henderson. Went off as soon as he saw him drive away."

"He didn't follow him home, though?"

"No, sir. Lambert was without a car last night. He came by bus, and was met by a woman at the bus stop. She'd arrived a few minutes before, in a taxi. The two of them took up a position opposite the garage, watched until Henderson came out and then went off together."

"Any idea who she was?"

"Never seen her before, sir."

"Probably just pointing the murderer out to the girl friend," said the inspector. "Showing her the man he hopes to help put away."

"Constable Peters says the woman was about forty."

"Bit old for a girl friend, you think? Maybe."

"And Peters says they both looked pretty down in the mouth."

"Did they now? I don't suppose Peters saw where they went?"

"No, sir. He had no instructions to keep them under observation."

"No, of course not. I just wondered. Well, if there's anything in it I expect we'll find out before we've finished."

"Yes, sir," said the sergeant.

In the course of that evening and the next day Terence told himself fifty times that the chances were that nothing would come of the affair, that Henderson would not even be arrested, let alone brought to trial. After all, he argued, the police would need a lot more evidence than what they were getting from him before they had a case against Henderson, and there was nothing at all to show they had anything else on him. Fifty times he reached that comforting conclusion, and fifty times his thoughts circled back to that identification parade and his spirits dropped to zero again. Because if the police had had a reason, entirely separate from anything he knew or could contribute, for including Henderson in that, if he had indeed been the man they hoped to trap, then the evidence he gave might be all they needed to clinch their case, and Henderson would surely be arrested.

So he waited all day, listening to every news broadcast,

buying each successive edition of the evening papers, dreading to hear the announcement that an arrest had been made. At ten o'clock that evening, when he had heard nothing all day, he rang the police station and asked what was happening. The official voice was bland; they were "following several leads," "hoping a pattern would emerge soon," "keeping in touch with various developments" and so on. Terence was so anxious for comfort that he clung to the expression "several leads"; he persuaded himself that even if an arrest were made it might not necessarily be Henderson they would put the finger on. The matter could in fact be cleared up without involving Terence himself any further. After all, in cases like this the police often took hundreds of statements and used only a fraction of them. "The police have interviewed hundreds of people in their hunt for the murderer." He must have seen that sentence dozens of times in the crime news. With the help of these reflections, and of several stiff whiskies, he was able to go to bed in a reasonably sanguine frame of mind.

Very early the next morning, however, the police arrested Chris Henderson and charged him with the murder of Toni Edwardes, the girl who had been found dead earlier in the week. According to the papers she was a nurse.

Sylvia saw the paragraph as soon as she picked up the evening paper. The brief statement had been framed in a box on the front page and printed in heavy type. Sylvia supposed that was because of the interest the series of attacks had aroused. With a sinking heart she realized that this would be a cause célèbre, one of the crimes of the century. After all, people still talked of Jack the Ripper, of the brides in the bath, of Christie. Chris Henderson's trial would be written up as theirs had been; it would be reported, discussed, published in book form. Terence's evidence would be printed, repeated, analyzed. It seemed to Sylvia, looking back longingly on their uninvolved days, that they had embarked on this increasingly perilous course with incredible lightheartedness. How pathetically childish of them to think they could cheat the system, tell lies and get away with them! Sitting there staring at the black headline, Sylvia felt an enormous apprehension on Terence's behalf. She also felt profound relief that she would not be standing up in court to give evidence. That would be the ultimate disaster. She discovered within herself a steely determination to have nothing further to do with the matter. It was not her affair; she would not be dragged into it. As the first step in her disengagement, she screwed the paper up and took it out to burn with the rest of the rubbish in the garden incinerator.

Terence's reaction was very different. His heart gave a great leap when he saw the report but when the first shock had subsided he felt strangely calm, much calmer than he had been for a long time, since before that night in January when all this business had started, or so it almost seemed, because he dated his troubles back to then. There had been a faint uneasiness underlying everything ever since Sylvia had wakened him with a scream. After that night it was as though they had been on a seesaw, wondering if anything would happen, just what would happen, but now doubt and uncertainty had been removed. What he and Sylvia had agreed would be the worst thing to happen had happened; Chris Henderson had been arrested, partly because of the information Terence had given the police; he would be tried and Terence would have to give the same (partly false) infor-

117

mation on oath. That was the position, and now it was inevitable Terence found himself accepting it and making plans for it. The first thing he did was to cut out the report of Henderson's arrest and put it away carefully. He had this instinct to make a dossier of the case, to collect and collate every possible scrap of information, and the announcement of Henderson's arrest was the first tangible item. The curtain had gone up, the drama would be played through to the end.

What Terence failed to appreciate was how long the prologue to that drama would be. Henderson was remanded three times, and nothing else happened for seven weeks. Terence, being ignorant of law, was unprepared for this hiatus and he was therefore unable to explain it adequately to Sylvia. She became furious, miserable and apprehensive when it dawned on her that the ordeal would not be over for months.

"You mean to say," she said incredulously, "that there's got to be a hearing in the magistrate's court first? And then a trial? And you'll have to stand up and give that evidence twice?"

"If they want me to, yes."

"Will they want you to?"

"Probably. Almost certainly."

"How will you know?"

"They'll send me a summons. A subpoena."

"And you'll *have* to go?"

"Look here, Sylvia, we've been over and over this. *Yes*, I have to. They could send me to prison if I didn't."

"They could send you to prison anyway, for perjury."

"For heaven's sake, Sylvia, can't you bloody well talk about anything else?"

This conversation took place over cups of tea in Terence's flat. The warmer weather had come at last, with the long light evenings, and the two of them were seated on either side of a small table in front of the open window. In the sunny square below, the plane trees in full leaf obscured the lower floors of the houses opposite and hid the stretch of footpath where the man had attacked the girl. The tea had been Sylvia's idea. On the bus coming over she had suddenly decided that a cup of tea was just what she felt like. She had got off at the next stop and bought a packet of her favorite brand, and on second thought a teapot—Terence's bachelor habit of a teabag in a cup held no appeal—and she had arrived at Terence's door with these homely objects in her hand. Now, in an effort to change the conversation, she asked him if he liked the tea.

"It's all right," he said.

Her face fell. "Only all right?" she asked.

"You know I like coffee," he said impatiently.

"You drink tea sometimes," she said.

"Look, if all you want to do the whole evening is to sit around and drink tea, why didn't you just stay at home and drink tea out of your own teapot in front of the telly?"

"I'm sorry," she said, and stood up and began to clear the cups away.

"Don't be so bloody ridiculous!" he cried, jumping up in his turn and barring the way to the kitchen.

"Let me past," she said, pushing against him. He stood his ground and one of the cups fell and broke.

They made it up, of course, mopping up the spilled tea, picking up the fragments of china together. They even went to bed, and afterward they made arrangements to meet again before the end of the week although they both knew that they would quarrel again. That was the pattern of their meetings these days. One or both of them would flare up over some little thing, then there would be a reconciliation followed by bed. Their lovemaking had a desperate quality now; they clung together, two frightened people reassuring each other. The gaiety, even the happiness, had gone out of their relationship, but the passion remained; they quarreled, but they were closer than they had ever been, they needed each other more. But in different ways. Sylvia needed to see Terence continually to assure herself that nothing had really happened. Terence was still there, not whisked away to some limbo, he still wanted her, she could still get to see him as often as ever. Perhaps nothing need ever change. Terence, on the other hand, tried to be with Sylvia as much as possible because she knew everything, yet she knew he was not really doing anything wrong. They therefore contrived to see each other more frequently than ever, sometimes as often as three times a week.

Sylvia still went to considerable lengths to deceive Edgar and Marion; she would have hated either of them to guess the truth. She hardly bothered any longer, however, to give Julie explanations for her frequent absences, her hurried telephone calls, her fits of preoccupation. Her excuses, when she gave them, were perfunctory and unconvincing. Neither she nor Julie ever said anything openly, but there was a tacit understanding between them. Sylvia felt this clearly, and she was sure Julie did too. Julie had changed again. She had got over her rebellious phase, she was once again a good girl, conforming and obedient, but she was obviously not happy; she talked of nothing but leaving school that July, which was now only a few weeks off. She no longer wanted to go to the university or to any kind of college; she was restless and moody and spoke of leaving home, but she had no definite plans at all. Normally, Sylvia would have been very worried about her. As it was, when Edgar spoke anxiously about her, Sylvia said lightly, "Oh, she can go and be an au pair for a year or so in France or Germany or somewhere. After all, lots of girls have a few months on the Continent between school and university, or work."

When Sylvia said this, Edgar was incredulous. "You mean you'd let her go?" he asked.

"If she wants to."

"This summer? But she's too young to go gallivanting off to Europe on her own."

"She's seventeen, that's not so young nowadays. And going off to live with a family is hardly gallivanting."

"But you were against even sending her to a boarding school."

"Oh, Edgar, that was quite different! She was only a child then, and anyhow she wanted to stay with us, but now she's nearly grown up and she wants to get away—you must have heard her say so a hundred times. So all I'm doing is trying to find something that appeals to her and that we'd feel happy about too. And it seems to me au pair work might very well be just the answer. It's a marvelous opportunity for a girl to get to know another country and learn a foreign language really well. You have to admit, Edgar, that languages are terrifically important."

"I don't have to admit any such thing," said Edgar crossly. "You're talking absolute rubbish, Sylvia, and I can't think what's got into you, letting Julie go off God knows where on her own. If you do that, you'll be washing your hands of her, that's what you'll be doing. She might end up somewhere bloody awful, just taking off into the blue like you apparently expect her to."

"You're being ridiculous," she said. "Naturally I shall be *extremely* particular about where she goes; I'll find out all about it before I'd even consider letting her go."

"How are you going to do that?"

Sylvia had mentioned au pair work almost at random, without thinking the matter through, but now that the idea had been brought out into the open she realized how much it appealed to her as a solution to the problem of Julie. Besides, Edgar's skepticism was a challenge. So she said, "I'll go to one of those agencies that advertise in the *Times,*" and the following day she did just that, and came home with a list of addresses. It seemed that in every country in Europe there were families wanting an English girl to live with them. Sylvia sat down straightaway, and eliminated those which were obviously unsuitable, then considered the others more carefully. In the end she settled on one in Athens as being the best all-round proposition.

"Athens!" said Edgar when she told him that night. "Greece! Let me see that list." He took it, and read it with angry concentration. "What about some of these in France?" he demanded. "Or Germany? At least she'd start off with a knowledge of the language."

"The idea is to *learn* a language," said Sylvia.

"*Greek!*" he said. "Modern Greek! What good will that do her?"

"You never know," said Sylvia. "Sometimes it's an advantage knowing an unusual language, one that hardly anybody else knows. When it comes to interpreting, and jobs like that.

122

I mean, everybody knows French and German. What's the use of spending your time on them?"

"Here's a job in Brussels," said Edgar. "And one in some town in Holland. At least she'd be able to get home for the occasional weekend if she took either of these."

"The family in Holland has six children," said Sylvia. "Julie would be run off her feet. And as for coming home on the weekends, that's no good. She'd never settle down if she knew she could get home so easily."

"I said the occasional weekend, not every weekend," said Edgar. "And how is she going to get home at all, from Athens?"

"The job's for a year," said Sylvia. "I expect she'd be entitled to some time off after six months. They might let her come home for a few days at Christmas, for example."

Edgar looked at her. "And you'd be quite happy to have Julie away in Greece for a whole year?" he asked.

"If that's what Julie decides she wants to do," said Sylvia. "I'll talk to her about it in the morning."

When Sylvia spoke to her after breakfast, Julie tried at first to maintain the sullen, uncooperative attitude she had adopted toward her mother, but it was no use, she was too interested. The thought of living abroad for a year was irresistible; she agreed to everything, and only wanted to know how soon she could leave for Athens. Recent differences were forgotten as the two of them went over the delights of a Mediterranean country—grapes, figs, sun, beaches, islands and ruins and wine and fishing—so that when Edgar arrived home he found that everything was as good as settled. He was angry and upset. He declared that he absolutely forbade Julie to go, and although this reduced Julie to tears and hys-

teria and Sylvia to tight-lipped irritation, he at first refused
to give his reasons, merely saying several times over that she
was not going, and that was that. He made it clear that as far
as he was concerned the self-evident absurdity of the whole
project made comment unnecessary, but he was not able to
maintain this position in the face of the others' combined
attack, and in the end of course he gave in. After that, things
moved with great rapidity. It was only three weeks to the
end of the school year; the Greek family wanted Julie to
come as soon as possible. Less than a month after the subject
had first been mentioned they drove Julie out to the airport
to take a night tourist flight to Athens. Julie wept, Marion
wept, Edgar was nervous and worried. Sylvia stayed calm
and bright. She found the right queue, she checked each
piece of luggage, she bought magazines for Julie to take, and
she kept talking cheerfully until it was time for Julie to leave
them and to go through to the departure lounge. Even then
Sylvia kept smiling and led the others up to the observation
deck. Although they watched eagerly they didn't see Julie
again, but they saw a Trident leave at the scheduled time and
felt sure she was aboard. Sylvia felt a searing flash of desola-
tion, a physical sense of loss, as the beautiful plane soared off
the tarmac and headed steeply for the clouds, but within a
few minutes relief reasserted itself. She had got rid of a potentially hostile witness; no chance now that Julie would tell
Marion or Edgar what she knew.

To Sylvia's surprise, Terence was almost as disturbed as
Edgar was about Julie's departure for Athens.

"Do you mean she's gone already?" he asked. "Who *are*
these people she's going to be living with, anyway?"

"There's no need to take that tone," she said. "Edgar and

I have gone into everything most carefully, and if we're satisfied I'm sure you should be. After all, what's it to you?"

"She's your girl," said Terence. "Surely that makes her mean something to me. And when all's said and done, Athens is a hell of a long way away. Doesn't it worry you at all, to think of her stuck down there on her own?"

"Of course it worries me," said Sylvia, changing her ground. "It worries me to death, but do you know why I let her go? It was for our sake, yours and mine. She'd begun to guess about us and I was afraid it was only a matter of time before she said something to Marion or Edgar. Of course, she couldn't have *proved* anything; I could have denied it all but it would have been very unpleasant. So when Greece came up I thought it was a good idea."

"It didn't exactly come up. It was your idea from the beginning, wasn't it?"

"I don't know why you're going on like this," said Sylvia. "Surely you can see how awkward it might have been for us, having her around any longer?"

"Not awkward for me," said Terence. "I don't care who knows about us. I never have, remember? All this secrecy is your idea, and now you've even sent your own daughter away for a year to preserve it."

"Julie wanted to go!" Sylvia cried.

"Oh, sure," he said, with irony.

The night before the court hearing Sylvia was at Terence's flat, "cheering him up," as she put it, and he said to her, "You *will* be there tomorrow, won't you, to give me moral support?" He had avoided asking her before, because he was nervous about her answer.

Sure enough, she took her time about replying, bending her head sideways away from him and stroking the back of his hand with one forefinger. "Sweetie," she said at last, "would you think it awful of me not to come?" She risked a quick glance at his face and went on hurriedly before he could say anything. "I know you've been thinking I'll be there, but really, is there any point? I mean, you say yourself it'll all be quite straightforward, so you won't need much in the way of moral support."

"I'd like you to be in court, though," he said, speaking as calmly as he could, but he could not entirely suppress a pleading undertone. "I've thought all along it's as though the two of us will be giving evidence. I'm the mouthpiece, but I'll be speaking for both of us."

"What are they going to ask you about, then?" she said fearfully. "You've been saying they are only going to ask questions about that time in Fortescue Street. I wasn't there, was I? How do you mean you'll be speaking for both of us?"

"But, Sylvia," he said, "I wouldn't have been in Fortescue Street in the first place if it hadn't been for what you told me you saw the other time. It's all bound up together. That's what I mean about the evidence being both of ours."

"Nobody knows about me, though," she said stubbornly, "and I don't want to go to court. I'd rather not."

They went on talking, but Sylvia remained obstinate. She would not go and watch proceedings. Instead she stayed at home and read the papers. Terence was not called until the second day and when Sylvia saw the report of his evidence she was amazed at how brief and simple it was. Yes, he had been in Fortescue Street on the night in question. Yes, he had seen the accused there. Yes, he had known who he was. And that was virtually all there was to it. Sylvia immediately thought he had been making a great fuss about nothing. Goodness, if she had realized how little was involved in this giving of evidence she would not have bothered to be so sympathetic. Privately, she felt that Terence had been over-estimating his importance as a witness. Surely those few ordinary little sentences had very little significance. In fact, for half an hour or so she felt decidedly flat, but when she thought about it she came more and more to realize what a good thing it was that Terence's evidence was so unsensational, and by the time she could ring him in the evening she was jubilant.

She insisted on coming round to the flat "to celebrate," and talked and behaved as if the whole matter was over and done with, and the trial itself just a tiresome formality as far as Terence was concerned. He had given his evidence in public now and they had believed him; all he had to do was to stand up in another, rather similar court and tell the same story and be believed again. That was all there was to it.

Terence listened to her in growing bewilderment and frustration. He tried to explain to her the difference between giving evidence at a preliminary hearing, and being a witness at a criminal trial; he warned her about what would happen when he was cross-examined. Sylvia refused to believe a word of it. She said he was being an alarmist. He brought out the newspaper reports in an attempt to prove to her just how vital his evidence was, but she wouldn't look at them.

"Oh, Terence"—she laughed—"you're being ridiculous. You're worrying about nothing at all."

Terence was baffled. Sylvia was not a stupid woman but she

was certainly behaving like one, and her refusal to face reality placed an additional strain on him during the weeks that followed. For she would not allow him to be low-spirited or apprehensive or even serious and quiet. As soon as he fell silent she would try to rally his spirits and laugh him out of it. He supposed she thought she was helping him but the result of her relentless frivolity was that he had no one to confide in.

When it was announced that the trial would be in late September Sylvia remarked gaily that in that case there was nothing to stop them from going away and having a good holiday "like everybody else." She didn't mean together, of course. The Mansons had booked months ago for two weeks at a seaside hotel in August. They had had to cancel Julie's room, but Sylvia and Edgar took Marion away with them as arranged. The glove factory closed down for the holidays and with Sylvia away there seemed little point in staying on in town as far as Terence was concerned. Acting on impulse, he walked into a travel agency's office one morning and arranged to leave on a conducted tour at the end of that week. It was going to places he had hardly heard of and had never thought about in his life but it was the only tour he could get on at such a late date. In any event, he quite enjoyed it; there was something soothing in being borne mindlessly along, told where to eat, what to see, when to stop and rest. He had not been so thoroughly looked after since he had left home at the age of seven to go to boarding school. He ate enormous meals, fell asleep as soon as his head touched that night's continental feather pillow, and sat in the sun as often as possible. At the beginning of the tour he felt and acted like a convalescent. By the end of the first week he was feeling decidedly better. During the second week he spent most of his time with one of the several single girls in the party. For her as well as for him it was just one of those holiday things, no future in it but fun while it lasted. He did not write to Sylvia. They had agreed not to because of the risks involved and he was glad of the excuse.

Once he was back in London, the tour rapidly receded into the past and became a tiny, sunlit interlude. For the rest of his life he found it hard to believe that he had ever been to any of those places.

So much for August.

When they met again in September, Sylvia surprised Terence by announcing that this time she would go to the court.

"But why?" he asked. "When you were so dead against it last time."

"I was silly," she said. "I didn't know what it would be like, and I was frightened. But now I know there is nothing to be frightened about."

"There never was anything for *you* to be frightened about," he said.

"Oh, I was frightened for your sake," she assured him. "Not for mine."

"And now you're not frightened about what will happen to me any more?" he asked.

"Of course not, silly!" she said. "What could happen to you?"

Terence, who had so much wanted her to be at the earlier hearing, was extremely reluctant to have her watching him give evidence at the trial, but he felt he could hardly say so. He listened with growing uneasiness as she wondered aloud who would be there and what she would wear and how much publicity the case would get.

"Anyone would think you were going to a bloody play!" he burst out one time, and she had not denied it. Instead, she had admitted that she couldn't help looking forward to it and regarding it as an absorbing piece of entertainment.

"You're morbid," he said crossly. "You're like one of those dreadful women that knitted beside the guillotine."

"I'm not like that at all!" she exclaimed. "I couldn't bear to see anyone even sentenced to death, but that doesn't happen these days. But naturally I'm frightfully interested in this case. After all, as you said yourself, I'm involved. Why shouldn't I be there?"

"Of course there's no reason why you shouldn't be there," he said, "but what worries me is that you obviously haven't the faintest idea what it's going to be like. I couldn't stand watching you being grilled, and you won't like watching it happen to me."

"You'll stand up to them," she said confidently. "You'll see, you'll be all right."

The trial opened on the last Tuesday in September. Public interest in it was intense, and Sylvia got up at dawn to queue for a seat. After deliberation she had told Edgar where she was going. There was after all nothing to link her with the case or with Terence. Edgar could suspect no motive other than curiosity. Predictably, he disapproved of her going and he made much the same objections as Terence had.

Sylvia was indignant. "It's not unhealthy to be interested in a case like this," she said. "It's unnatural not to be. I don't know why you are all being so critical about my wanting to go to the trial."

Edgar raised his eyebrows. "All?" he said. "Who else is objecting?"

"Oh, some of the women at the club," said Sylvia, improvising. "And the newspapers, of course. They are always printing disapproving remarks about women who go to trials."

"I quite agree with them," said Edgar stiffly, but Sylvia was totally unmoved. She knew from long experience that Edgar always took the conservative point of view and that he liked women to be ladies. The idea of his wife struggling for a place in the gallery at a murder trial was bound to be distasteful to him, but she was determined to go and that was that. So she shrugged her shoulders and set the alarm for five o'clock in the morning.

Marion was astonished that anything could get her mother up so early. She came down in her dressing gown to the kitchen when Sylvia was having tea and toast and showed a belated curiosity about the whole case. Sylvia found it very odd to be discussing the imminent trial with someone who was so completely uninvolved. She had to be very careful not to give away too much but apparently she succeeded, because Marion was not at all suspicious and in fact soon lost interest.

Sylvia drove the car up to the city early and found a place to park but when she arrived at the court there was already a queue waiting. She spent the next few hours wondering if she would get in but when the doors opened she was borne along in the rush and found herself safely wedged on one of the benches inside. After all this preliminary excitement, however, that first day in court was rather dull. Matters of procedure were settled, lawyers argued, policemen and doctors gave their technical evidence. There were moments of pathos, as when the dead girl's clothing was displayed in court, or when her elderly father gave evidence of identification, but no high drama. Gradually, though, as the day wore on, Sylvia found she was increasingly caught up in the story which was unfolding before her. Items which earlier would have seemed utterly commonplace were revealed as essential links in a chain and by the end of the day she was totally gripped by it all.

Sylvia thought she might have seen Terence outside the court but there was no sign of him, so she rang him that evening. He was distinctly curt on the phone and not at all inclined to gossip about the proceedings so far, as Sylvia wanted to. He said that all he knew of the trial was what he had read in the papers that evening, but when she pressed him he admitted that he expected to be called as a witness the following day.

Even so, it came as a shock when she heard his name called in court: "Terence Hugh Maudesley Lambert." She had forgotten the Maudesley—he had been named for his father's general. And when he came in he looked small and somehow insignificant, so that Sylvia felt what she had never before felt toward him—protective. She sat forward tensely and stared down at him but when he began answering the questions his voice was clear and confident and Sylvia gradually relaxed and found she was able to listen to his evidence with as much interest as she had to what the others had said.

The first questions were routine, the answers easy, and the prosecutor took Terence briskly through them, but when the preliminaries had been disposed of, the pace slowed and became more deliberate. Truth was being stalked in the courtroom; the hunter was delicately circling, drawing nearer. . . .

The lawyer began by getting Terence to describe how he had seen Chris Henderson in Fortescue Street on the night of the murder. This, although important to the case, was straightforward and not sensational. The questions and answers were crisp and matter-of-fact; the court listened quietly. The bridging question, the one designed to lead on to the next point, followed so naturally on the ones before, was slipped in so smoothly, that even Sylvia didn't recognize it for what it was, although she had been waiting for it.

"You say you recognized Mr. Henderson because he worked at the garage where you used to take your car," the lawyer began conversationally; then, "Had you ever seen him anywhere else—besides in Fortescue Street, of course?"

"I'd seen him round quite a bit," said Terence, and the caution in his voice alerted Sylvia to danger.

"Where, for instance?"

"In Jellicoe Street. And at the garage where he works."

"Jellicoe Street being where the Hendersons live. And where else have you seen the accused?"

Sylvia held her breath. Here it was, the moment when Terence had to lie to the assembled court, to the suspicious lawyers and the busy clerks and the remote and silent judge. The obstinate and obtuse confidence of recent weeks fell away from Sylvia, and she was as nervous and frightened as she had been at the beginning. But diagonally across the court from her Terence appeared unmoved, though still watchful, and he answered this question as calmly as he had the others.

"I saw him in Birdwood Square," he said. "In January."

"Birdwood Square being where you live. What date in January?"

"The sixteenth."

"What time?"

"In the evening. About a quarter to eleven."

"Can you remember what Mr. Henderson was doing when you saw him?"

At this point there was a stir in court, and consultation between the lawyers and the judge, but after only a brief delay Terence was directed to answer.

"I was looking out of my window," he began.

"Your window overlooks the square?" the lawyer put in.

"Yes, it overlooks the square, and I saw a man and a girl walking along the other side."

"Together?"

"No; the man was behind the girl, and as I watched he sprang at her."

"You mean he attacked her?"

"Yes, he attacked her."

"What happened?"

"The girl screamed, and the man ran away."

"And the man whom you saw attack this girl?"

"He was Chris Henderson," said Terence firmly.

"The man whom you knew from the garage?"

"Yes."

"And the man whom you saw on the night of the eighteenth of May in Fortescue Street?"

"Yes."

"And you are quite sure you saw the accused on both these occasions?"

"Yes," said Terence again. "It was the accused I saw both times."

"Thank you, Mr. Lambert," said the prosecutor, and sat down with a flourish.

Theoretically Terence knew the procedure, he expected to be cross-examined, yet when the prosecutor sat down with such an air of finality Terence turned to leave the witness box and had to be recalled to face counsel for the defense.

The lawyer was a small man, and he began mildly, even conversationally.

"Let us start," he said, "with the alleged encounter in Fortescue Street, since what happened near that street is what concerns us here. Mr. Lambert, you say you saw the accused in Fortescue Street on the night of the eighteenth of May?"

"That's right."

"You were walking along the street and you saw this man?"

"No, I was in a car."

"You were in a car and you saw this man walking along the street?"

"He was in a car too."

The lawyer looked up in apparent astonishment. "You were both inside cars? Driving along, or stationary?"

"We were both driving along the street."

"Let me get this clear, Mr. Lambert. You were driving along Fortescue Street, and you thought you saw the accused in a passing car?"

"I did see him, but not in a passing car. We were going in the same direction. I was following behind him."

"You were behind him? Did he turn around at any point?"

"I don't think so."

"And this was at nine o'clock at night?"

"About that."

"Is the court to understand that you were driving along a street at night, and you saw the back of a man's head in the

135

car in front of you, and on the strength of that you are prepared to stand up in a court of law months later and swear to that man's identity?"

"It was the accused I saw," said Terence. He sounded foolishly stubborn, and Sylvia looked across at the jury to see if they believed him, but their faces were as expressionless as a row of puddings.

"Of course," counsel for the defense was saying, and now his quiet and soft way of talking seemed sinister and sly, "you are good at identifying people under difficult circumstances. Isn't that so?" Terence was silent. "Isn't that so, Mr. Lambert?" the lawyer repeated, his voice sharpening a little.

"I don't know," said Terence. "I don't know what you mean."

"You don't know what I mean? Let us go back, Mr. Lambert, and consider what you have been telling this court." He stopped and made a show of shuffling his papers. Terence lifted his head so that the light fell full on his face. Sylvia thought he might be looking for her and she gave a tiny wave, which was all she dared do, but she had no way of telling whether he noticed. The examining lawyer straightened himself with a sheet of paper in his hand, and Terence turned obediently to face him again.

"Now, you were in your flat in Birdwood Square on the night of the sixteenth of January, and you looked out of your window and you saw a man attack a girl. Is that right?"

"Yes."

"Which window?"

"The bedroom window."

"So you were standing at your window, and this girl and this man came into sight?"

"No, when I looked out of the window they were already in sight."

"They were already in sight? The man at one end of the street and the girl at the other?"

"No; the first I saw, the man was right behind the girl, and just at that very minute he attacked her."

"So you just happened to look out of your window just as the man attacked the girl? What did you do then?"

"I called out."

"You didn't run down to the street?"

"No."

"And the man, what did he do?"

"He ran away."

"As soon as you called out?"

"Yes. Really, it all seemed to happen at once."

"It all happened at once. You mean you saw these two people, the man attacked the girl, you called out and the man ran away, and all this seemed to happen at once? Is that what you mean?"

Terence plainly hesitated, and Sylvia caught her breath. Suddenly there was danger.

"Not literally all at once," Terence said.

"But very quickly indeed?"

"Everything happened quickly, yes."

"How quickly? How long do you estimate all this took? Come on, Mr. Lambert—five seconds?"

"Longer than that, of course."

"Ten seconds? Twenty seconds?"

"It must have been more than that."

"Must have been? Did it seem more than that, then?"

"I told you, it didn't seem long, but for all those things

to have happened it must have been longer."

"A lot of things can happen in twenty seconds. But let us just say that you saw this man for a brief and fleeting period of time. Did you then get in touch with the police?"

"Not that evening."

"So it was not that evening that you gave your famous description to the police?"

"No."

"When was it?"

"I don't remember the exact date," said Terence, but he was hedging. Sylvia knew it, the lawyer knew it, and he waited until Terence went on. "It was in March," he said, "after another girl was attacked."

"March—that would make it at least six weeks later, and possibly more?" He waited until Terence had agreed, then pressed him further. "So after a gap of about two months, you went to the police and you gave them what you alleged to be a detailed description of a man you had seen for only a few seconds? And now, weeks later again, you are prepared to swear that a man you saw only from the back in a moving car was the man you had described to the police?"

Terence didn't answer, and Sylvia found herself gripping her hands together and wondering why the police had put Terence on the stand and exposed him to this humiliation. Because, without the missing links, his story was ridiculous. She wanted to call out to him, to tell him to go back, to start again, to include everything so that the tale made sense. But there was no going back, no chance to fill in the gaps, and counsel for the defense had not finished yet. He was speaking again. Dear God, what was he talking about?

"Mr. Lambert," he was asking, "how far would you say it

was from your bedroom window to the other side of the square?"

"I haven't any idea."

"Would it surprise you to hear that it is approximately forty-three yards?"

"I suppose that would be about right."

"That would be in a straight line from your window to a point directly opposite. Now you have told the court that this alleged attack took place at the junction of the square and Melton Street, which runs into one corner of this square. Another thing—what is known as Birdwood Square is in fact an oblong, a rather long, narrow oblong. You would agree with this description?"

"Yes, fair enough."

"So that the distance from your window to the Melton Street corner is farther than the distance straight across the square from your window?"

"Well, of course."

"Would you accept that it is in fact more than twice as far?"

"I expect you've measured it," said Terence.

"We have measured it, Mr. Lambert, and we have found it to be ninety-two yards. Ninety-two yards. Now let us move on. The night of the sixteenth of January was of course a winter's night. Was it a fine night, Mr. Lambert?"

"I don't think it was, particularly."

"It was in fact a damp and misty night?"

"It wasn't raining, it was frosty."

"And foggy?"

"There may have been some fog around."

"At all events the visibility was not good?"

"There are streetlamps," said Terence, and Sylvia remem-

139

bered the lamps with the fuzzy halos of light. The lawyer was right; it had been foggy.

"Thank you," said the lawyer. "I was coming to the lights. There are three of them, aren't there, spaced along the far side of the square from your flat?"

"Yes, there are three that side. The square is really quite well lit."

"You'd say that, would you? As well lit as the High Street?"

"No."

"As well lit as this courtroom?"

"No, of course not."

"Of course not." With a sudden movement that swirled his gown around him, counsel for the defense turned to look up at the judge, and Terence, Sylvia and most of the others in court turned too. "My lord," said counsel, "with your permission, I'd like to try a little experiment."

The judge leaned forward. "Is it relevant?" he asked.

"I think so, my lord."

"And it will not take up much of the court's time?"

"Only two minutes at the most, my lord."

"Please go ahead."

"Thank you, my lord." The lawyer faced Terence again. "Mr. Lambert," he said, "I have in my hand an object." With great deliberation he raised his arm above his head and held it so, with the palm facing outward, then spread his fingers out, to show what he was holding. "Mr. Lambert," he said, "would you kindly tell the court what this object is?"

By straining her eyes, Sylvia could tell even from where she was sitting that it was a small red notebook that the lawyer was holding aloft. She could not imagine what the significance of such a notebook could be, and she waited in a fever of impatience to see what Terence would say about it. But Terence said nothing at all, while the court waited.

"Come on, Mr. Lambert," said the lawyer, after perhaps half a minute, "what is this? Is it a handkerchief? A cap? A lady's slipper?"

There was nervous laughter in court but Terence was still silent, and for a panicky instant Sylvia imagined the notebook as hiding some dreadful secret, then it dawned on her that the explanation was simpler—Terence just could not see what the lawyer was holding up, even though he was straining forward and peering across at it with the most desperate intensity.

The lawyer was relaxed and smiling now. He knew he had won. "Please answer," he said. "It's not by any chance a red *wig* I'm holding, is it?"

"I can't tell what it is," said Terence at last. "I can see there's something there, but I don't know what."

"You can't identify it, in fact?"

"No."

"Not at a distance of only seven yards, in a brightly lit room? How long is it since you had your eyes tested, Mr. Lambert?"

"Some years."

"And what were you told about your eyes? Were you told for example that you were shortsighted?"

"Yes."

"Were glasses prescribed for you?"

"Yes."

"Were you wearing these glasses on the night of the sixteenth of January?"

"No. Actually I only wear them at work."

"But you are in fact extremely shortsighted?"

"I don't know about extremely."

"Mr. Lambert, don't trifle with the court. Would you not agree that a person who failed to distinguish an object from a distance of only a few yards could fairly be described as extremely shortsighted?"

"I suppose so."

"And not at all the kind of person likely to be able to identify someone over ninety yards away on a dark and misty night?"

There was a flurry of objections, in the midst of which Terence was dismissed from the witness stand. Sylvia watched him step down, and felt both bewildered and very worried. The lawyers were conferring, there was a whispering among the spectators, Sylvia had the uncomfortable feeling that everyone in court understood better than she did what had happened. She wanted to get away and if possible to see Terence, but she was suddenly nervous of making herself conspicuous by pushing past the other spectators, so she sat on until the court rose.

She tried to explain this to Terence when she rang him that evening but he refused to understand her point of view.

"You might have guessed I'd want to see you," he said several times, "to ask you how you thought it went."

"I thought you were quite good really," she said, but without conviction. He was not reassured and after a while they lapsed into dejected silence. "Perhaps it will turn out all right," was the most she could offer.

But it turned out badly. The trial lasted for the rest of the week, and at the end of that time the jury deliberated for less than two hours before acquitting Chris Henderson, who therefore left the court a free man.

"But they can't blame you," said Sylvia that night at the flat. "Can they?"

"Blame me for what?"

"For the fact he got off scot-free. Your evidence wouldn't really have made any difference, would it?"

"Of course it would have." In a queer way he felt offended. "They were relying on it. If it had come off it would have shown that Henderson had tried to do in another girl a few weeks before."

"But you did see him in Fortescue Street. That part of it was true."

"So what? There's nothing wrong with being in Fortescue Street. As far as that goes, I was there myself. Henderson says himself he was there. All I was saying is that I saw him where he said he was."

"There's nothing wrong in *your* being there. You never attacked a girl in the street."

"As far as the police are concerned neither did Chris Henderson, which brings us back where we started from. They found him not guilty, you know, Sylvia, and we've got to face up to the fact that he mightn't have done it. We mustn't lose sight of the fact that I *didn't* actually see him in the square that night. I mean, that damned lawyer made a fool of me, all right, but he only brought out what was true all along, that I had no right identifying someone I hadn't seen."

"But *I* saw him," said Sylvia. "And there's nothing wrong with my eyesight."

"There can't be," said Terence slowly. "Now I come to think of it, you're actually longsighted, aren't you? I mean, you don't have any trouble reading bus numbers and street signs and all that sort of thing. Could you see it was a note-book he was holding up?"

"Easily."

"So if you'd been the one giving the evidence he wouldn't have caught you like that."

"He probably wouldn't have tried," said Sylvia shrewdly. "He must have been pretty confident you'd flunk the test or he wouldn't have risked it."

"How could he have known, though?"

"He probably noticed you peering at something—or wait a minute! Where do you keep your glasses?"

"Nowhere special. I usually leave them in my drawer at work, now that I rarely drive." He broke off and they looked at each other. "He couldn't have done that," he said. "He wouldn't have been allowed in. Nobody at the office would have let him poke round among my things."

"Oh, Terence!" she said. "I'm frightened. Supposing he bribed someone?"

"Well, never mind all that now," he said with an effort. "It's all over; there's nothing we can do about it. The best thing we can do is to forget the whole thing, just say, O.K., so he didn't do it."

"But, Terence," said Sylvia, dropping her voice, "if he did do it, he can now go off and do it again. And really, you know, I'm sure it *was* him."

"You're not to go round saying that!" he said angrily. "You've got no proof!"

"I have so!" she cried. "I've got the best possible proof. You're forgetting, I *saw* him."

"You told me you weren't sure it was him. I asked you that time up at the garage, I *begged* you to tell me one way or the other, but you wouldn't. You said you were not sure."

"But I am now."

"How can you be? If you weren't sure months ago how can you be so sure all this time later?"

"I *am*, though," she said obstinately. "When I saw him in court I was certain he was the man I had seen down in the square." And nothing Terence said could shake her.

When at last Sylvia had gone, and he had calmed down sufficiently to review the situation from all angles, Terence realized he had no idea what, if anything, would happen next. The words "A man can't be tried twice for the same crime" came into his mind pat as a quotation, and he wondered if they were true and what they really meant. Presumably if they meant anything they meant that Henderson could never be tried again for the Fortescue Street affair, but other girls had been attacked and murdered. Did the police have enough evidence to arrest Henderson in connection with any of these other crimes? But surely if they had had any such evidence they would have had it in reserve this time, to bolster up the case when it sagged. So would they now watch Henderson night and day, hoping he would become careless and reveal some connection with any of those other crimes? Or perhaps they would watch him, hoping sooner or later to catch him in the act of committing still another crime? Or maybe they would shrug their shoulders and accept the verdict.

But Terence didn't think they would. All right, so he had let the side down as a witness—it was hard to avoid sporting terms—but they had had other things to go on. Some of them he knew about. There had, of course, been the other evidence given at the trial, little bits and pieces of information, none of them particularly significant in isolation, so that Terence found it hard to remember the various items separately.

The whole case against Henderson had been built up like a picture, with tiny, careful strokes, and the discrediting of Terence's own evidence had pulled the whole pattern crooked. Terence resolved to get a written transcript of the trial as soon as possible, so that he could evaluate the meaning and importance of everything that had been said and stated. In the meantime, he turned his attention to other points.

Why, for example, had Henderson been included in the identification parade? Certainly not on Terence's own flimsy evidence, which at that time had amounted to no more than a suggestion that a red-haired man was involved. They *must* have suspected him on some other evidence—but then Terence saw the flaw. All except one of those twelve men must have been selected on chance, why not Henderson? The garage was not far from the police station. One of the men there could very well have known of the red-haired mechanic who could conveniently be included in the lineup. And this unwelcome thought led on to another. In the early weeks of his affair with Sylvia, when he still had his car, they must have stopped at the garage more than once. When Sylvia looked at Henderson now, she thought she remembered him from that night in Birdwood Square; might she not rather have recalled his face from one of those stops at the garage? These thoughts flapped round in his head like bats, until he felt physically stifled and escaped down to the street for a walk and some cool night air.

When he came reluctantly back in, the phone was ringing. He picked it up and felt a great surge of weariness when he recognized Sylvia's voice.

"Terence, is that you?" she was saying. "Where have you

been? I've been trying to get you for the last half hour."

Terence forced himself to speak calmly. "What is it?" he asked. "Nothing has happened, has it?"

"No, but I'm so worried, I had to ring. I've been thinking. . . . Terence, you don't think you'll get into trouble over all this, do you?"

"Trouble?" he said, and couldn't keep an edgy note out of his voice.

She knew he was annoyed, and spoke timidly. "About your evidence. It wasn't really true, was it?"

"It never was. Remember?"

"I know it wasn't, but then they went on and proved it couldn't possibly be true." She stopped, but he was silent and she had to go on. "So I can't help wondering if they are going to do anything about it."

"*Do* anything about it? Arrest me, you mean? For making a mistake? Don't be ridiculous!"

"But, Terence," she persisted, "it wasn't just a mistake, was it? I mean, it didn't even *sound* like a mistake, either, saying all that when you couldn't even see him properly."

"For God's sake, Sylvia," he cried, "whose side are you on, anyway?" He regretted his words as soon as he had spoken them; they sounded childish and panicky. He took a deep breath to steady himself and forced himself to speak calmly. "They'll think I saw the outline and imagined the rest," he said. "Wrong identification is very common."

"They'll be furious all the same."

"They won't be pleased," he admitted. "I'd better watch my step for a few weeks, otherwise they'll be down on me like a ton of bricks, trying to get their own back."

As a joke it fell flat, and Sylvia ignored it. "Terence," she said, in a different tone of voice that made him realize she had come to the point of her phone call, "you won't say anything about me, will you, whatever happens? I won't be brought into it, will I?"

He could not stop himself from saying, "So it's yourself you're worried about, not me?"

"Of course I'm worried about you," she said, too quickly. "I'm worried sick about you. I'd hate anything to happen to you."

"But you'd hate it even worse if you were involved?"

"That's not fair," she said. "After all, it's only natural to think about these things."

"I suppose so," he said, not wanting to quarrel, but he felt a little chilled just the same.

"So he got off, sir," said the sergeant to the inspector. "Makes you wonder whether it's all worthwhile."

"Never say die," said Inspector Quirke. "Bring me the files."

"I take it we're reopening the case then," said the sergeant.

"Reopening it? It's never been closed."

When the sergeant brought the files the inspector said, "Get yourself taken off everything else. I want you free for the next few days so that you can get around and see some of these characters again."

"Lambert, sir?"

"Lambert for one, but not just yet."

"While I think of it, that woman of his was in court the first two days."

"The one Peters saw with him at the garage? Was she now? Came to see him give evidence, eh?"

"I'd say so, sir."

"Any idea who she is?"

"Peters happened to see her drive off. He made a note of the car number and looked it up. Just out of curiosity, you might say."

"And?"

The sergeant flipped open his notebook and found what he wanted. "Registered in the name of Manson, Edgar James."

"So there's a fair chance this woman is Mrs. Edgar Manson?"

"I'd say so, sir. Peters says she has her fair share of rings."

"Observant lad, Peters. There's probably nothing in it, but give him the chance of following it up."

"Sir?"

"Send him round to these people, let him see if it is the same woman and whether she's this Manson's wife. No questions, of course, just a spot of quiet checking."

Terence knew the people in the other flats in his building by sight though not by name. He knew that in the flat immediately below his there lived a rather pleasant middle-aged woman. She lived alone; for some reason Terence had always assumed she was a widow. They exchanged formal greetings when they met on the stairs or in the entrance hall but never anything more. It was therefore a surprise to Terence when one day about a week after the trial this woman stopped him on the landing outside her door and said, "Mr. Lambert, I wonder if you could spare a moment?"

He already had his foot on the bottom stair going up. When she spoke, he brought it back down onto the landing and turned to face her.

"Of course," he said, too warmly, to cover his surprise and

149

the awkwardness of not knowing her name. How had she learned his?

"At first I didn't know whether to say anything or not," she was saying, "but it seems only right you should know. I don't want to go behind anybody's back."

What could she be talking about? He assumed an attitude of polite attention but his thoughts were racing, and he missed a few words.

"But at first I couldn't remember," she was saying. "It's so long ago, but I did see the people all gathered round the girl, and then the next day Mrs. Mullins over at the corner shop told me what it was all about and so I knew then."

Mrs. Mullins at the corner shop indeed, he thought savagely. Linkups everywhere. They might just as well be living in a village. "Who's been talking?" he asked. "Who has brought all this up again?"

"The *police*," she said, amazed he did not know, and in fact he found he had known; her answer had been the only possible one.

"You mean they've been talking to you about it today?"

"Yesterday."

"Did they say why, after so long?"

"No, but I suppose something's turned up," she said vaguely. "Anyhow, as I was saying, they asked me if I'd seen you that night at all."

"Seen me?" He tried an incredulous laugh.

"Well, at first I thought I hadn't. You *were* home, of course, but the police knew that already from what you said at the trial"—his name and address in all the papers; no wonder she had known what to call him—"but I explained how there wasn't much coming and going between these flats so nobody knows about the others."

"So you said you hadn't seen me?" He was too quick.

"I did at first, but then I remembered how I just peeked out when I heard you coming up the stairs, to see who it was. I'm always nervous at night."

He glanced at her door. Like his, it had a glass panel. "So what did you tell them?" he asked.

"Why, just that—that I saw you when you came back in."

"Fancy remembering," he said. "I wouldn't have had a clue whether I went out that evening or not." In fact, if he had been asked, he would probably have replied, quite innocently, that he hadn't been out at all. Going with Sylvia to get her a taxi was such a trivial thing, a bare ten-minute excursion.

"Wouldn't you?" she said, and it was hard to make out her tone. "But you do know you were home for part of the evening, because you saw that girl attacked." Obviously she had read the reports of the trial, and evidently she believed his evidence. Didn't she realize he had been proved a liar, or at best mistaken? Had she read the reports inattentively, over a cup of tea, or was it that she was loyal to a neighbor, even in unneighborly London? Was she just a little bit stupid, or was she potentially his friend and ally? He would have to try to find out.

"And you say I went out later?" he asked with what he hoped sounded like cheerful indifference.

"Oh, you *did*," she assured him. "When Mrs. Mullins told me the next day about the girl I thought that was where you must have been the night before, over the road with the others, but then at the trial you said you hadn't been over near the girl at all, and when I came to think of it, it was a bit later when I saw you, after all the excitement had died down."

"I expect I'd just dodged out for a breath of fresh air."

"Something like that, I daresay." It was dark on the landing. Terence could make out the glint of the woman's pearl earrings but her face was in shadow, and he couldn't tell her expression, but he sensed reserve in her voice, and he was uneasy. Just how soundproof were these flats? Her bedroom immediately under his, only a few feet separating their windows—the London anonymity he and Sylvia had relied on seemed to be dissolving fast. And then he recalled that she had said she had seen him *coming back in.* Did that imply she had also seen him going out? If so, she would have seen both of them, Sylvia and him together, and he felt obscurely that this would be a safeguard, that the fact of Sylvia's presence would serve as a protection against something he did not care to formulate. He had to know whether he had this protection.

"Did you see me going out?" he asked, as casually as he could manage.

She dashed his hopes. "Oh, no," she said. "I just saw you the once, going up. After eleven, I suppose it must have been."

He felt her watching him, as though the time were significant, as of course it was. It was probable that unless he involved Sylvia he would not be able to prove he was home during the early part of that evening. This woman knew that he had been out after eleven. The girl in the square had been attacked about ten-thirty. The other girl had been murdered between leaving the tube station at ten to eleven and being found at ten past midnight.

Terence had been uneasy; now he was frightened.

The woman—he would have to find out her name—was

still talking. "So I'm glad to have had this chance of telling you about it," she was saying.

"That's all right," he said mechanically. "I don't suppose we'll hear any more about it."

"Probably not," she said, opening her bag and taking out her key. "Good night, Mr. Lambert."

He hesitated, unsure whether to go on up or to wait until she had disappeared into her flat, but she settled the matter by giving him a nod of dismissal and turning her back, leaving him free to retreat up the stairs and consider his position. He thought about it all evening but came to no definite conclusions. Sylvia was coming round the following day and he became impatient to tell her that the police were asking questions again, partly because he longed to discuss it with someone and she was his only confidant, and partly from a rather spiteful desire to ruffle her irritating complacency.

But the next day when she came she was so gay, so light-hearted in a way she had not been for months, that he could not bear to shatter her mood but instead surrendered to it. Sylvia all glowing and happy was irresistible in a way Terence had almost forgotten she could be and in spite of himself he was swept up into her euphoria. From wanting to tell her about the police he came right around to dreading she might guess that anything could still be wrong. Because for this evening at any rate all Sylvia's doubts seemed to be resolved, her fears dispelled. She had been worried in case the police took some action against Terence, she had been nervous about getting involved herself, but a week without incident had been enough to set her mind at ease. She was now convinced that everything was over.

"And really," she told Terence, "it's all worked out for the best. Let's face it, if that man had been convicted mainly on your evidence, it would have been rather frightful. As it was, we did all we could, and no harm came of it. There's nothing we can reproach ourselves with, looking back."

Terence had thought that Sylvia would want to forget the trial as much as he did, but instead she kept on returning to it, lingering over all sorts of details, like the hats the women jurors had worn and the way the judge had kept on coughing. She was like someone who, having negotiated a difficult passage, turned back to survey it at leisure from a safe vantage point. Terence, listening to her, realized that this would be one of the exciting events of her life, the time when she was involved in a famous murder and had seen her lover giving evidence at the trial. Terence wondered if he would ever be able to view it in such simple and romantic terms.

He asked Sylvia about Julie. Sylvia answered briefly that she had got over being homesick and that she was liking Greece better now that it was not so hot. Terence then asked her what she had been doing since he saw her last. She replied vaguely that she had been doing some shopping.

It sounded reassuringly innocuous. "No outings?" he ventured.

"Not unless you count lunch in town with an old school friend. That's all right, isn't it? You're not jealous?"

He played up to her teasing. "I happen to know they were all girls at your school. Thank goodness. Been doing any entertaining?"

"Do we ever?"

"No visitors at all?"

"Not a soul. Unless you count the policeman yesterday."

"The policeman?" he said, suddenly sobered. "What policeman?"

She noticed his agitation and said, "I felt a bit like that too when I opened the door and saw him standing there."

"What did he want?"

"Oh, nothing, really. Something about the car, whether it was registered, I forget. Edgar was home, so he dealt with it, whatever it was."

"You haven't had an accident with the car or anything?"

"Of course not. I told you, it was something to do with the registration."

Terence felt uneasy, but he told himself he was being ridiculous. All the same, a policeman asking questions at the Mansons' at the very time that other police were interviewing people in his neighborhood—that surely was an ominous coincidence.

To his annoyance, Terence saw his neighbor in the downstairs flat again the following day. Two meetings in three days —Terence was sure she must have been watching for him, although she pretended surprise when they met on the pavement outside. He now knew her name, having taken the trouble of looking at the letters in her box. Miss Eves, so not a widow after all.

"Oh, Mr. Lambert!" she exclaimed. "Good morning."

"Good morning," he returned, meaning to say just that and walk past, but she was looking at him expectantly, and he weakened. "Out early today?" he remarked.

"Oh, I'm usually earlier than this," she said. "I'm running a bit late this morning."

"I mustn't keep you then," he said. He had been right; she'd been laying in wait for him. He sidled past her, but she called after him, even put a hand out to stop him.

"Mr. Lambert, before you go, do you remember what we

155

were talking about the other day? Those visitors? They've been round again."

"The police have been to see you again?" he asked. She blushed at his plain talk and gave a quick glance around, but there was nobody near. "They didn't come to see me," she said, with an indefinite note in her voice—reproach? regret? "It was the Mullinses they came to see. Mrs. Mullins said they asked a whole heap of questions."

"About that girl, I suppose."

"About her, but about the people around here mostly. Mrs. Mullins says there wasn't much she could tell them because the people round here keep to themselves." *Or used to,* Terence commented sourly to himself. "One thing they asked her was did she know anyone in these flats, and when she mentioned me they were quite interested because you know how you called out? Well, apparently some woman called out too. Mrs. Mullins herself didn't hear a thing, she was in bed, but one of the men who ran out into the street definitely heard a woman's voice calling out from this direction. So that means someone else must have seen what happened besides you and the police want to find out who it was. It's hard to think who it could have been. I don't know of any other woman in a flat looking out this way, do you?"

"It mightn't have been from these flats."

"Where else could it have been from? The man was quite certain it was from over here. But it's funny the woman hasn't come forward, isn't it?"

"There was no reason why she should," said Terence. "That's if there was a woman at all. The girl wasn't really hurt."

"But with all the publicity?"

"That came later. She'd probably forgotten all about it by then."

"I wouldn't have forgotten," said Miss Eves. "A girl practically murdered right outside my window! I'd remember every single thing about it for the rest of my life."

It was three days later when the police came to see Terence himself. Inspector Quirke and the sergeant, very genial, very friendly.

Terence felt obliged to apologize for his failure in court.

"Lawyers' tricks, Mr. Lambert," said the inspector. "We're used to them."

"I still think that chap had red hair, you know," said Terence, out of an obscure desire to justify himself, but as soon as he had spoken he was exasperated at having mentioned it. Better by far to have let it go.

No chance of that now. The inspector was on to his assertion like a terrier. "Do you still think it was *Henderson*, though?" he asked. "That's the point."

"I'm absolutely convinced of it." Terence was so desperately anxious to establish his sincerity that he spoke with too much emphasis and the tone came out false to his own ears.

"If it was Henderson all the time," said the inspector, "that's that. Unless we get him on something else."

"I suppose you'll keep an eye on him for a while?"

"That depends," said the inspector, but he didn't go on to say what it depended on. "In the meantime, Mr. Lambert, we'll have to cast around for other leads. That means more questions, I'm afraid."

"I don't mind," said Terence. "Fire away."

"First of all, then, let's get this straight. You knew Henderson because he worked at the garage where you used to take your car. Right? How long ago did you start taking your car in there?"

"About three years ago. A bit longer, even."

"And you sold your car when? About Christmas?"

"A couple of weeks before Christmas."

"So you'd been taking your car into that garage for something over two years? You'd therefore known Henderson for that length of time?"

"I suppose so, but only vaguely. The only reason I knew him at all was that he happened to be the one who generally did my car."

"How often would he have worked on the car?"

"Christ, I don't know." The inspector waited. "Eight or nine times perhaps."

"And you saw him each time? Would you have spoken to him?"

"Probably, but only a few words. He isn't what you'd call a talkative chap."

"So to sum up, you saw and spoke to Henderson on a number of occasions. How was it then that you didn't recognize him when you saw him attacking the girl?"

"How could I?" Terence demanded. "It was months since I'd seen him, it was dark, he was across the street—how could I possibly have identified him?"

"But that's just what you did do. You did identify him."

"Not right off. That was after I'd seen him several more times. When I saw him again it just clicked that he was the chap I'd seen. And don't forget I definitely did see him in Fortescue Street. There's no doubt about that, is there?"

"You say it 'just clicked' when you saw him again. Would

that have been at the identification parade?"

"I was pretty sure when I saw him there, yes."

"But you didn't say anything?"

"It shook me that it was someone I knew."

"So you waited until another girl was murdered," said the inspector. His voice was factual, devoid of expression, but Terence flushed.

"Do you think I haven't thought of that?" he demanded.

The inspector made no comment. He was busy taking some papers out of a folder. "Let's see how you are on dates," he said pleasantly. "I've got some written down here, and I'd like you to try to remember what you were doing on each of them. The sixteenth of January," he went on, almost as though talking to himself, "and the eighteenth of May. Well, we know where you were on those two days, don't we? Now, how about the seventeenth of October?"

"The seventeenth of October? Last year? I haven't a clue."

"The third of December?"

"Look, that's ten months ago. You can't possibly expect me to remember offhand what I was doing on that particular day."

"Do you keep a diary, Mr. Lambert? Any sort of engagement book?"

"Not a book. There's a calendar at the office I sometimes write things on. Business appointments mainly. Or when I have to see my dentist."

"Does the third of March ring any bell with you?"

Terence hesitated. "Wasn't that when I got in touch with you the first time?" he asked, but he was being disingenuous. He knew he had rung the police on the fourth. A girl had been attacked on the night of the third; he had answered vaguely because he found he had a strong reluctance to showing the police how precisely he remembered everything about that night. "I forget," "I don't remember," "I don't know"—he felt instinctively that safety lay in such replies. Only the honest citizen with nothing to hide could afford to cooperate unhesitatingly with the police.

On the sixteenth of January, one girl had been attacked in the square and the au pair girl had been murdered. On the third of March, another girl had been attacked. On the eighteenth of May the nurse had been killed in Fortescue Street. Terence suspected the other two dates, in October and in December, were equally significant. He would have to find out for sure, but not by asking Inspector Quirke. In front of him he dared not show any concern.

When he was alone, he hunted through old papers in his closets. In the morning he searched the library files, but both times he drew a blank. The dates were too long ago. Although he could not prove it, he was, however, quite sure that a girl had been attacked on each of these dates. Which suggested another nasty little riddle. At the time of the last murder, the papers had made a great deal of the fact that there had been seven earlier attacks on girls in that district. Seven known attacks. As he knew, there had been at least one other that they were not counting. That made eight attacks that the police could have questioned him on. Take away the two he had come forward and given evidence on, and that left six. Why then hadn't the police asked him about six dates, instead of only three? Several disagreeable possible reasons presented themselves to him. It would have been much easier to dismiss the questioning as routine if it had been less selective.

On arriving back at the office from the library the following morning, Terence found a note on his desk asking him to see the manager. This was not at all unusual. The financial state of the glove factory was by then so shaky that Terence was having long, anxious sessions with the manager several times a week. So Terence picked up his books and went in, prepared to explain yet again that the sales were just not high enough. He expected to find the elderly manager hunched as usual over charts and reports, but the desk was clear of papers and the manager was over by the window looking out. When he heard Terence come in he turned around but didn't speak, merely nodded a greeting.

"You wanted to see me?" Terence asked, resting his books on the bare desk top.

The manager hesitated, then seemed to come to some sort of decision. "Yes, I did," he said, extra briskly, as though to make up for his initial fumbling. "I wanted to tell you I've had the police here."

Terence knew he should show surprise, startled interest, coupled with a lack of personal concern, but such dissembling was quite beyond him. He felt sick in his stomach, incapable of acting casually. "The police?" was all he managed to say.

"Two of them. A detective inspector, no less. And a sergeant with him. The inspector said he'd been to see you at home. Name of Quirke."

"That's right."

"So you'll know what it's all about. Eh?"

"Yes," said Terence. His voice came out thick and unfamiliar. He cleared his throat and forced himself to continue. "It's that case I was mixed up in, that girl who was murdered."

"The chap got off," said the manager. "I'd have thought that would be the end of it as far as you were concerned."

"I wish to hell it was. But they're making inquiries all over again. What sort of questions were they asking here?"

"Well, first they wanted to know what the business was that took you over to that side of town the night the girl was murdered."

Terence did not take it in at first. He looked up, puzzled, a little confused, and found the manager was looking at him with great intentness. He became apprehensive. There was something here, something dangerous. . . .

When Terence didn't answer, the manager began to elaborate. "According to this inspector you told the police you were over there on firm business that night. I said it was the first I'd heard about it."

Terence literally felt the blood draining from his face, leaving his skin cold and clammy. Everything the moralists had ever said about lies was being proved true. Right at the beginning, at the very first interview, he had accounted for his presence in the street by saying he had been there on business. They had not asked him how he had come to be there; he had volunteered the explanation, hoping to make his whole story more convincing by filling in a plausible background and he had without really thinking about it repeated to the police an excuse for his actions that he had previously used with Sylvia. They had not remarked on it at the time, it had not been brought up in either court, it had never been referred to again, yet they must have noted it down, and all the while the lying sentence had been there, buried in the files, waiting to be isolated, brought out and analyzed. . . .

Terence realized the manager was looking closely at him,

waiting for his reply. He licked his lips. "I couldn't have said that," he said. "They must have made a mistake, misunderstood something I said."

"I wondered about that," said the manager, "but they told me they've got it all written down and signed that you were over there on business to do with your job here. I told them straight that there was no sort of business that could have taken you over to that side of town, let alone at that hour of night."

"Hang on," said Terence. "There was, you know. I've just thought—round about then we were pretty worried about those accounts, remember? And now I come to think of it, I did go chasing some of them up myself. I could have been doing that."

"What accounts?"

"Some of those damned shopkeepers. A couple of them have places over that way."

"Which ones?"

"Jesus, how would I know? I looked up their names and addresses at the time and I know there was at least one somewhere over there, but that was months ago, after all."

"This was at night. You say you went calling at this shop at night?"

"Not calling. I wanted to take a look in his window, see what sort of stock he was carrying, size him up a bit before I started to put the pressure on."

"Another thing," said the manager. "What the hell's the idea, driving all over the place in one of the firm cars?"

"I'm entitled to the use of a car, aren't I?"

"Not at night you aren't, and not without signing the book, as you know damned well."

"How the hell do you expect me to chase up these characters, then?" Terence blustered.

"I don't," said the manager bleakly. "You can save those stories for the police. Don't try them out on me, and don't you go dragging the firm's name into your private affairs either, do you hear me?"

"You can keep your bloody firm," said Terence. "That's gratitude for you, when you think of all the unpaid bloody hours I've put in, trying to save you from going down the drain."

"Lay off the firm, I told you. At least we've never had the police here before."

"It's only sheer bloody luck you haven't, the way it's been run."

"Are you resigning, Lambert?"

"Are you giving me the sack?" The words seemed to echo round the little office, and the men stood rigid, as though listening to the reverberations. Then gradually they relaxed, became confused. The tension drained out of the atmosphere, leaving them tired and muddled and a little ashamed.

The manager was the first to recover. "Let's leave all that in the meantime," he said, shrugging. "No point in doing anything in a hurry."

Terence hesitated, then began to pick up his papers. He found his hands were shaking. "I'll be getting back then," he mumbled, head down, and made for the door. Back in his office, he dumped everything, flopped in his chair and lit a cigarette, but found he was too shaken to smoke it all the way through. He stubbed it out, put his head in his hands and gave way to great tearing waves of panic. He could no longer blind himself to the obvious. The police suspected him of murder. It was ridiculous, grotesque; it should have been easy to shrug off, but he found that to be stalked as a murderer had a paralyzing effect. He became a hypnotized rabbit. It was humiliating. He struggled to account for it. Perhaps if he had not been conscious of the lesser guilt of perjury, he would have been able to rebut suspicion more convincingly. But because he had lied he had areas to conceal. Frankness would have been his best weapon but he could not afford to be absolutely open.

It was while he was sitting there, with his head in his hands, besieged by these thoughts, shaken by his scene with the manager—for the old man had always been good to him—that the revelation came, and like all revelations, once it had been made it was blindingly self-evident.

Sylvia would be his salvation.

He sat up and went over the points with mounting excitement. Sylvia could give him a cast-iron alibi for that first, crucial assault, and in the process she would explain away every one of those discrepancies that had led the police to suspect him—the business of the identification, why he hadn't spoken sooner, and all the rest of it. With that cleared up, he would be able to tell them how he had come to be in Fortescue Street on the fatal night and how it was that he had known it was Henderson in that car. That would be enough to show the police that he was innocent, but there was more. On the night of the March attack Sylvia had been with him; she had rung him the next morning with the news about the girl. They had not been together that evening in May when the girl had been murdered, but with any luck they could have been at the flat on any or all of the crucial dates. That would be extra, though, not necessary. Once Sylvia had made her statement about the sixteenth of January nothing more would be needed to clear him absolutely. That would be the end of the affair as far as he was concerned. The police would take no further interest in him; he would be of no conceivable value to them as a witness now that Henderson had been tried and acquitted and neither would Sylvia. Now it was perfectly safe for her to come forward and tell the truth. No danger of her having to stand up in court and tell it in public —Henderson's trial was over and done with. Sylvia had only to have a brief private talk with the inspector and it would all be over, all the worry and the nightmare. And it had all been so unnecessary.

He tried to ring Sylvia immediately, and at intervals throughout the afternoon, but there was no reply. He tried to imagine what she could be doing—shopping, visiting, going to a matinee. Everything he thought of seemed incredibly trivial; that she could be concerning herself with such everyday things when he wanted so desperately to talk to her was monstrous.

He rang again as soon as he got back to the flat, going straight across to the phone without waiting to take his coat off, and this time Sylvia answered. She took the call with Marion in the house and Edgar expected back any moment, and consequently she was nervous and inattentive. It took her a few minutes to grasp that Terence was insisting on seeing her that very evening, as soon as possible. She demurred and made difficulties. He was peremptory and she gave in, but it was after nine before she came, though she had promised to be there by eight.

She arrived sulky, full of grievances, but he gave her no opportunity to complain. He was watching for her, came down to meet her, hurried her up the stairs and into the flat, talking to her all the way, explaining how things were, outlining what he wanted her to do. He went much too fast for Sylvia; she did not understand. Indeed, she could not seem to get past the fact that the police had been to see him again.

"You mean they've been around here since the trial?" she demanded. "They've been asking you more questions?"

Terence was impatient. "I've just been telling you," he said. "But the point is, it doesn't *matter*."

"It doesn't matter! What do you mean? Of course it matters! Don't you realize they're probably going to arrest you for perjury?"

In the circumstances, this was so funny that Terence laughed. He had come a long way from when a charge of perjury was the worst he had to fear. "It's not perjury they're interested in," he said. "It's murder."

She waved her hands impatiently. "Well, of course," she said, "but if they're coming to see you again it must be because of the evidence you gave at the trial. Obviously."

"No," he said. "You are wrong. The fact is, they have come round to thinking I might be the one they want for the murders." He shrank from saying the word "murderer" even to Sylvia.

She, however, had no such scruples. "You mean they think you're the murderer?" she demanded, and the robust way she spoke the word showed that the possibility had no reality as far as she was concerned.

"It's crazy, of course," he said apologetically, "but you can see how they got the idea. It's a case of a lot of little things adding up to the wrong answer. Rather terrifying in a way, but easy enough to put right." He was eager to go on and tell her how she could save him, but she interrupted him before he got any further.

"But you must be mad," she said, with an incredulous little laugh. "They would never think a thing like that! You a murderer? Whatever next?"

"They *do* think it," he said, brusque, impatient, anxious to get past this elementary, self-evident point and on to the solution. "But, Sylvia, I'm trying to tell you, all we've got to do to get them off my back—"

She interrupted him again, no laughter this time. "Terence, you *are* mad. You can't be serious."

"Damn it all!" he said. "I tell you, they are busy building up a case against me and it's got to the point where they've practically got one. They've been going over everything with a fine-tooth comb, they've gone round to the neighbors asking questions, they've even been to the office. Last night they were asking me where I was on the various nights the girls were attacked. They haven't been any too subtle about it, you know—they suspect me all right."

Sylvia was staring at him. "But that's terrible!" she said, in a small, muffled voice. "That's just terrible."

He frowned, irritated at having to spend precious time in allaying her quite unnecessary panic. "I do wish you'd listen," he complained. "I've been trying to tell you it's *all right*. They suspect me because I didn't tell the truth in court. Oh, for other reasons as well, but that's what put them on to me in the first place. They think because I lied I must have something to hide."

"But you said before that they wouldn't think you were actually lying," she said fearfully. "You said they'd just think you'd made a mistake."

168

"Never mind all that now," he said. "Perhaps I said that, but it doesn't matter. The point is, when I was standing up in court I couldn't tell them the whole truth because I *did* have something to hide, but that something wasn't what they thought it was. So all I have to do is to tell them what I really was hiding, and they'll promptly lose interest in me."

"I don't understand," she said. "What will you tell them?"

"Why, the truth, of course, but it would come better from you."

"The truth? You mean about us?"

"About you being here that night, and seeing Henderson."

"I'm not sure it was Henderson," she said obstinately.

He waved this aside.

"The man, then," he said. "Now that's not much, is it? All you need to say is that you were here and looked out the window and saw the whole thing."

"No," she said, huddling down into her end of the couch like a wary animal. "No, I couldn't."

"Ah, come on, Sylvia," he said. "Who's to know? Only a policeman or two."

"Only!" she said.

"It's nothing anyway," he said. "Being in the flat, what's that? It wasn't late, not much after ten. We could always say we were having a cup of coffee or listening to records."

"Or looking at your etchings," she said scornfully. "They're not fools. They know that if that was all there had been, there would have been nothing to stop us from telling the truth in the first place."

"We could say that you were afraid your husband would misunderstand," Terence said. "All the publicity frightened

169

you. After all, standing up in court is quite an ordeal at the best of times."

"So you want me to go to the police," she said.

"It's the only thing to do."

"I won't do it," she said.

"But, Sylvia," he said, trying to be patient, "why on earth not? Are you afraid the police will be shocked or something?"

"Don't be silly," she said. "I don't care about the *police*. I'm not worrying at all about what they think."

This jarred on him. "Aren't you just!" he exclaimed. "Well, I am. Don't you realize, it's what they've been thinking about me lately that's the cause of all this trouble."

"Why do you twist everything I say?" she complained. "You've been saying all along that I shouldn't care what the police think, and when I say I *don't* care you turn on me."

He was silent for a minute, steadying himself before replying. He reminded himself there was something in what she said. He was letting his irritation get the better of him. He must keep calm. "I'm sorry," he said. "The trouble is, I've been pretty damned worried these last few days, with the police hounding me the way they have been."

"Hounding! What sort of word is that? You're exaggerating, as usual."

"They've been hounding me," he repeated firmly. "Padding along behind me. And it wasn't until this afternoon that I realized I could call them off any time I wanted. It took me that long to realize I have a cast-iron alibi, which just shows how jumpy I'd got."

"What do you mean, you've got an alibi?"

"Well, you know I have!"

"You mean you want me to give you one?"

"It's not a case of giving," he said, annoyed. "You *are* my alibi. It was you I was with, remember?"

"Terence," she began, in a cold resolute tone that made his heart sink, "right at the beginning we agreed that it was impossible for me to admit that I was here that night. That is why we went to all the trouble of arranging for you to give the evidence, wasn't it? And now after all this time, and after you've stood up in two courts and sworn twice over that you saw it all, *now* you want me to come forward and say it was me all along. Where does that leave me, for heaven's sake? I wouldn't have a scrap of reputation left. I'd be branded as a liar and a coward, and an adulteress as well."

For a fleeting moment, Terence considered lightening the atmosphere by saying, "Well, aren't you, darling?" but he dismissed the idea as soon as it occurred to him. He wasn't going to be able to tease Sylvia out of this. So instead he said, as gently as he could, "Listen, Sylvia, we can go along together, if you like, and we can say we both saw the man, then there'll be no question of my having told lies on oath, no danger of the police getting me for perjury. We can say we both saw the chap—we won't insist it was Henderson—and it was you who noticed the red hair, but you didn't want to give evidence. We can say that neither of us wanted to be dragged into the case, but later on, when we realized that what we had seen could be so important, we decided to contact the police on the understanding that I'd be the one to actually give the evidence. They'd buy that, I'm sure. It makes sense, and it's almost the truth. And another thing—those dates they've been asking me about. I can say I was with you

171

then too—you *were* here on some of them at least, and who's to know about the others, if I say you were here and so do you."

"But I couldn't do that!" said Sylvia, staring at him. "I can't say I've been coming to this flat for months on end, for more than a year!"

"Why on earth not? What difference does it make whether you've been coming here for one month or twenty?"

"You said before that we could say I had just dropped in for a cup of coffee. They won't believe that if we tell them I've been coming here regularly for so long."

He tried to laugh. "Oh, I don't know," he said. "Old friends chatting together over a cup of coffee. What could be more natural?"

"You are being idiotic," she said coldly. "Once and for all, Terence, I am not going to the police. Is that clear? I just can't do it."

"Won't, you mean."

"All right then, won't. Right from the beginning I've said I wouldn't go to the police, so I don't know why you're bringing all this up now. Especially since you completely agreed with me that I couldn't say anything."

"But things have changed," he said urgently. "Surely you can see that. The situation's quite different now the trial's over and Henderson has been acquitted. Before, your evidence would have been only against him but now it's for my sake, to save me, that you'd be giving it."

"So now it's for you you want me to admit that we've been having an affair."

"But only to a couple of policemen, Sylvia," he pleaded. "That's another difference. Before, you might have had to stand up in court and say it in public. That's one of the main reasons why I agreed that you couldn't really come forward. It would have been awkward."

"It would have been *horrible!*" she said vehemently.

"I didn't feel as strongly as that about it," he said, speaking very reasonably in an attempt to persuade her to be less emotional. "As you know, I've never been ashamed of our relationship; everything could have been brought out into the open as far as I was concerned."

"You had nothing to lose!" she flung at him.

"No, that's true," he said, still speaking with a great show of fairness. "The situation was more serious for you so I let you decide what to do, but now the position's completely altered. I'm the one who is in danger now, but you are absolutely safe. You can talk to the police without running any risk at all."

"That's what you think, just because it suits you to believe it."

"What risk is there?"

"Supposing the police go to Edgar and ask him where I was on all of those nights you're talking about?"

"Why would they do that?" asked Terence scornfully, but he felt a tremor of unease. If they really suspected him of such serious crimes they would certainly check any alibi he offered. They could very well approach Edgar, but he crushed that thought down as soon as it occurred to him. He had to convince Sylvia that it was necessary to tell the police almost everything, and that it was safe to do so, and to convince her, he had to be confident himself. "Look," he said urgently, "they'd take your word for it. They'd have no reason to doubt you. Damn it all, you'd be telling them the truth."

"Not like you," she said, "causing all this trouble."

"I did the best I could!" he said, stung. "It wasn't so far from the truth as all that."

"Far enough to have got us into this mess," she said.

"Shut up about all that, can't you?" he cried, and felt panic flickering in the background. Things were slipping further and further askew, just when he could not afford to have them go wrong. He controlled his anxiety and irritation as well as he could and set to work to soothe and persuade Sylvia, but he had no success. She grew more nervy and stubborn and refused point-blank to have anything at all to do with the police. In the end she became positively hysterical, so that he became alarmed, and to placate her he found himself promising not to mention her name under any circumstances.

Sylvia immediately became much calmer, and pointed out that he was probably imagining things anyhow.

"It's not as though they've said anything definite about suspecting you," she said. "Naturally they had to start asking questions again, they couldn't let the whole thing drop. What would the papers say if they did that? So they've begun by going round to all the people they've already interviewed, just to make sure they haven't missed anything. You can be sure you're not the only person they've visited this week, Terence, and I'm willing to bet that none of the others has jumped to the conclusion that the police suspect him of being the murderer. The only reason you have is because you've got a guilty conscience over that evidence you gave."

While Sylvia talked on in a similar strain, Terence listened with mixed feelings, including resentment at her patronizing tone and the stirring of a faint hope that she might be right. What she was saying was plausible enough; perhaps he was imagining things. He resolved to get a grip on himself and keep calm. When she smiled coaxingly at him and said, "Let's talk about something else," he made himself smile back and concentrated on following her lead.

After she had left—as he went with her down the stairs he wondered who was watching them—he tried to maintain a sensible and optimistic frame of mind and to a surprising degree he succeeded. He made and drank a cup of cocoa, fed the cat, had a shower, listened to the late news, and managed to complete each of these activities without giving way to an attack of nerves midway. He maintained his poise throughout the whole of the next day as well, which pleased him very much. By the end of the afternoon his fears of only twenty-four hours earlier seemed unreal, as though he had wakened from a nightmare to find that the things that had frightened him had never really happened.

It struck him as unfair, therefore, and a cruel blow, when he arrived home from work and found the inspector waiting for him on the doorstep. In spite of all his careful reasoning his immediate, panicky reaction was that he was there to arrest him, and when the inspector smiled deferentially and spoke politely he found himself straining to get past the smooth surface to the real meaning of his words. Gradually it dawned on him, first, that the inspector was saying it was just a matter of an extra question or two, and secondly, that the inspector seemed to mean what he was saying, that he was in fact merely going to question him again. He felt both relieved and ashamed—it was humiliating not to have his nerves under better control.

"Just home from work?" the inspector was asking. "Did you think to have a look at that calendar?"

"There was nothing there," said Terence. He was reluctant to admit he knew of the police visit to his office. The whole affair was like a game of cards; the less he revealed to his opponent the better. "I was thinking, though," he went on in what he hoped would impress as a frank, cooperative manner, "and I'm pretty sure I was home that night in March."

"By home, do you mean this flat here?" asked the inspector, and when Terence nodded, he said, "You don't go out much, then."

"Not during the week."

"You're not like the young lads today," said the inspector. "Never at home, some of them." He spoke feelingly, and Terence wondered if this was a chink in the armor, a glimpse of the inspector as a private individual. Perhaps he had teenage sons? But it was more likely to be a professional observation, young people racketing around at all hours, getting into trouble, making messes for the police to clean up.

Terence tried to decide whether the policeman's assessment had been accurate. Was it true that compared with most people he did not go out much? He couldn't make up his mind. Shaken up and jangling as he was, he felt unsure of the simplest things.

All this time the two of them had been standing on the landing. Becoming aware of this, Terence unlocked the door and stepped back, but the inspector waved him in first as though to emphasize that he was not there as a guest.

"And you live here alone?" said the inspector when they were standing together on the living-room carpet.

"I told you!" said Terence, his voice rising. "You asked me that once before and I told you. Yes, I do live alone. There's nothing wrong with that, is there?"

"Of course not," said the inspector mildly. "And I remembered what you said before, but after all, that was months ago. You could have had someone move in since."

"Well, I haven't," said Terence. The inspector made no reply to this, and there was a moment's awkward silence, long enough for Terence to regret having answered so brusquely, especially as he began to have a glimmering of how the inspector's question could be turned to good account.

"Sorry," he therefore said. "We might as well sit down, I suppose." They settled themselves, and Terence took out and lit a cigarette while he was wondering just how to phrase what he wanted to say. The first thing was to achieve a relaxed tone that would implant the idea deftly, so that the inspector would note it, yet casually too, so that he wouldn't give it undue weight.

"Of course," Terence began, as nonchalantly as possible, "the fact that I live alone doesn't mean I'm always on my own. I quite often have people staying."

"Relations?" suggested the inspector.

Terence shot a quick suspicious look at him, but the policeman's face was a bland mask. "I haven't got any relations to speak of," he said. "I was meaning friends."

"I expect you quite often put up out-of-town people," said the inspector. "Being so central and having the room."

This time Terence was sure the inspector was being willfully obtuse, but he had to play along with him, so he said, "I wasn't exactly thinking of that, either. I'd better come straight out and say I sometimes have a girl friend here."

"That would be a regular girl friend, sir?" asked the inspector.

Terence thought fleetingly of Sylvia. If he were to betray her, this would be the moment. But almost instantly he was shaking his head. "Good heavens, no," he heard himself saying, "nothing like that. Just girls, you know."

"Girls you meet at parties and pubs and so on?"

"Places like that, yes."

"Did you have one of these girls with you on any of the dates we're interested in?"

"That's just it," said Terence. "I can't remember."

"No diary?" asked the inspector, and smiled.

Terence laughed. "Not that sort of diary, I'm afraid. Too compromising."

"What about that famous night in January? Anyone here then?"

Terence held his cheerful expression with an effort while he rapidly considered what to say. His old mistake, not thinking things out far enough ahead. Danger lay in being too definite either way. He must leave it open. "Same applies, I'm afraid," he said, sounding rueful. "I just can't say."

The inspector raised his eyebrows. "You can't say?" he inquired. "You mean you don't remember? You saw this little episode, and you can't remember whether there was anyone with you at the time, anyone you discussed it with or pointed it out to?"

"I'm sorry," said Terence. "I can't be sure." It was not at

all convincing. In the circumstances he would certainly have remembered any companion.

But the inspector pretended to accept his word. "Ah, well," he said, "if you do happen to remember, you'll let us have the young lady's name, won't you. It could be helpful."

"Certainly," said Terence. "That's if I can manage to remember what she called herself," he added incautiously. He meant it as a joke, a bit of bravado, but the inspector failed to smile.

"What she called herself?" he repeated. "You mean you wouldn't know her real name?"

"I wouldn't know any name at all! Hang it all, it was getting on for a year ago!" and Terence was suddenly conscious of a real sense of grievance. "Who remembers things clearly as long ago as that?" he demanded.

"But you would have known the young lady's name at the time?" asked the inspector, unmoved. "That's if there *was* a young lady, of course."

"Well, of course I would," said Terence. "Why wouldn't I?"

"Quite usual, sir, not to know their names. Most of these girls call themselves something fancy. Honey Bear or Gaye Abandon, or some such."

Terence stared at him. "Did you make those up?" he asked, momentarily sidetracked. Then he realized the implications. "You don't think I bring *prostitutes* home, do you?" he demanded, genuinely offended.

"That's what I understood you to have implied, sir."

"Hell, I don't go picking girls up off the street."

"We did mention pubs, though. How about coffee bars or cafés?"

Terence hesitated. He had in fact met Sylvia in a tearoom.

She had been alone, and he had asked to share her table. . . . "Not in the way you mean," he said finally. "Not just casually."

"So you're not in the habit of accosting women?"

It was the legal word "accosting" that warned Terence. "Of course not," he said, and began to sweat as he realized the picture his idiotic posturing had been conjuring up for the inspector—a man living on his own, a divorced man not as young as all that, prowling round the streets at night, looking for women who were willing to come back to his room. Supposing such a man spoke to a girl, and she laughed at him or threatened to call the police, wouldn't he lose his temper? Or supposing such a man became disgusted with easy, cheap women and hankered after fresh young girls who would never even look at him, so that he grew to hate them, to want to crush and destroy them—" 'Say that she were gone, given to the fire, a moiety of my rest might come to me again.' "

Terence pulled himself up. It was sick, the way he was thinking. His clumsy attempt to hint that he might have had a companion, to indicate that he could have had an alibi, without involving Sylvia, had managed to suggest several possible motives for murder, but after all none of them was true. He reminded himself that he was only thirty-four and attractive to women, with an adequate if unconventional sex life and no possible reason for taking desperate measures to satisfy himself.

He took out his cigarettes, then noticed his fingers were shaking and clumsily stuffed the pack back into his pocket without taking one. Surely the inspector could see that he was normal, not a misfit or a psychopath? If not, perhaps it

180

was partly his own fault, because he had implied he had casual sex, but after all, wasn't that normal too, for a single man of his age? He had a sudden dizzy feeling that his view of the world and the inspector's were dangerously different, the inspector's being both more puritanical and more cynical.

The inspector had his head bent over his notebook but Terence was not deceived. He knew he was being observed closely, all traces of agitation noted. Now Inspector Quirke turned over a page and said, "When were you divorced, Mr. Lambert?"

For a minute Terence literally could not think when it had been, and when he pulled himself together and said, "Ten years ago now," he found himself stammering, which disconcerted him and surprised him too, because thank God there was nothing there that could be held against him. He had been the one who had been wronged; he had divorced Jenny on the good clean grounds of her desertion. "My wife ran away," he explained. "She left a note on the mantelpiece saying she was off to Birmingham with Fred."

"Fred?"

"Her boyfriend. He played in a dance band."

"And they're living in Birmingham?"

"God, no. Last I heard they were in Canada."

"Did they marry?"

"So I heard."

"So your ex-wife's name is?"

"Williams. He was Fred Williams. What's all this, anyway? What are we talking about my ex-wife for? I haven't even thought of her for years."

"You might call it a bit of checking in depth, sir," said the inspector. "The sergeant had you down as single, but I seemed to remember you had told us you were divorced."

Had he told them? It seemed unlikely, but he had no real idea. He decided to go on the attack, although one small cool part of his brain warned him he was behaving like a cornered rat. "See here, Inspector," he began as fiercely as he could, "are you picking on me because of what happened at the trial? Have you got a down on me because that bloody lawyer made sure nobody believed a word I said?"

"We don't know whether anybody believed you or not," the inspector said. "We have no way of telling what the jury accepts and it's what they believe that counts."

"They found him not guilty, didn't they?" demanded Terence savagely. "Does that look as though they believed me? Does it? Not bloody likely, and that's why you're snooping around, asking the neighbors about me, even showing up at the office. You're getting your own back because you think I let you down."

The inspector gave him a tolerant smile. "I expect it might look a bit that way," he said, "to anyone not used to our methods, but the fact is when a case is thrown wide open again, the way this one has been, we get out our files and we check each last little thing all over again, down to this word 'single' written against your name."

"But a divorced person *is* legally single," argued Terence.

"Legally perhaps, but to us there's a difference between 'never married,' and 'widowed' or 'divorced.' One party after all has connections, experiences, emotions, obligations that the other party hasn't. But I didn't come here to give you a lecture."

"What *did* you come here for?" asked Terence, deliberately rude. "Have I forgotten, or didn't you say?"

The inspector looked at him. "Mainly to ask about that calendar," he said mildly.

After the inspector had gone Terence went back over the conversation with a feeling of unreality. How on earth had they ever got onto divorce and the rest? He realized it had been the inspector's apparently casual question about living alone that had started it all. Was this chance, or had the inspector calculated his reactions? He asked the question, but he knew the answer. Nothing had happened by chance. It was a chilling experience, being interviewed by a professional. It was true he had not yet told the inspector about Sylvia, but he was no longer confident of being able to keep the secret indefinitely.

"We'll have to tell him," he said to Sylvia the following evening. "He's going to find out anyhow, and it'll be better if we get in first."

"Who says he's going to find out?" she demanded, whipping round to face him. "You've lost your nerve, that's what's happened."

Her face was very close to his, confronting him belligerently, and Terence found himself thinking she looked years older and harder. It even occurred to him at that moment that if he had ever seen her looking like that in the early days of their acquaintance they would never have become lovers. And then he was ashamed of himself, because after all it was not Sylvia's fault that worrying circumstances were aging her, and as an act of contrition he hastened to agree with her that he was probably overstating things and that there was after all no need to tell the inspector anything. "I probably won't ever see the chap again," he said with a hopeful smile, but Sylvia did not smile back. In spite of her scornful dismissal of Terence's fears, she could not convince herself that things would be all right.

Things were now going badly for her all round. Marion, for example, was making endless difficulties about her O levels, and was threatening to stop school the day she turned sixteen. Julie was writing tearful letters home begging to be allowed to leave Greece at the end of six months instead of staying for a year as she had agreed to do. She was coming home anyhow for Christmas and Sylvia found she was dreading the reunion because of all the arguments that would be bound to flare up—arguments, and very possibly accusations as well. She lay awake nights trying to devise schemes to keep Julie away, and then in the morning there would be another unhappy letter from the girl, and she would feel remorse and guilt.

Another worry was that Edgar was not well. Several times recently he had had migraine headaches and although the doctor prescribed tablets that alleviated the pain and even averted it altogether if taken at the first warning symptom, the sudden onset of the headaches worried Edgar and made him irritable and depressed, quite unlike his usual competent, unemotional self. Sylvia was worried too. In spite of common sense, she thought uneasily of brain tumors and strokes, early retirement and sudden death. She dreaded widowhood. She had seen too many women, some as young as she was, wither away under the loneliness of it, the loss of status, the financial problems. The possibility of being able to marry Terence if "anything happened" to Edgar never seriously entered into her calculations. She thought of it sometimes, of course, but only to dismiss it. For her, Terence

carried a bachelor's aura of freedom and gaiety, irresponsibil-
ity and charm, which was both an attraction and a limitation.
Because of it, she simply could not see Terence as a husband.
Edgar was her husband, and he was ill, and it was a gnawing
anxiety.

But the worst thing that happened during that time was
that the wife of Edgar's brother suddenly left her husband.
This brother was several years older than Edgar; he and his
wife were both in their fifties, with three grown-up children.
They were grandparents several times over, and for over
thirty years they had led an orderly existence in a big quiet
house in a quiet suburb. Edgar and Sylvia saw them several
times a year; the two couples exchanged formal, decorous
visits during which the men talked about business and their
gardens and the women compared recipes and shopping
hints. Sylvia's own family was outspoken, given to noisy quarrels and boisterous conversations and open displays of affection—in a rare comment years before Edgar had said that the
Glanvilles were always either shouting at each other or kiss-
ing each other—and this family behavior seemed normal to
Sylvia. She admired the Mansons for their politeness and
restraint, their habit of deferring to each other, but for years
she never quite believed in them. She kept on expecting an
argument, an outburst, a disagreement of some kind, but
nothing of the sort ever happened. The Mansons continued
to treat each other with an unvarying consideration which
Sylvia found rather intimidating. She consoled herself with
the reflection that they were able to behave impeccably only
because they felt nothing deeply. Their beliefs and their
emotions alike were correct, controlled and tepid.

This was true of Edgar as well as the rest. Years ago, Sylvia had resigned herself to the fact that Edgar, although an exemplary husband, was not a passionate one. He could not be goaded into losing his temper, but neither could he be roused to impulsive displays of affection.

"He even stops to put the trees into his shoes before he climbs into bed with me," Sylvia had complained to one of her sisters after a few months of marriage.

This sister, whose husband was always in debt and soon to be bankrupt, had been quick to point out Edgar's solid merits, but although Sylvia had to agree with everything she said, Edgar's restraint remained a prime grievance of hers right up to the time when she met Terence, after which it became a safeguard. Grievance or safeguard, however, Sylvia had long accepted Edgar's nature as set and unchangeable; she would have said she could predict his reactions to any situation.

She also quite expected that any drama would always come from her side of the family. Over the years they had had her brother-in-law's bankruptcy, a couple of broken engagements, a niece involved in an unfortunate love affair, a cousin fined more than once for speeding—none of them very serious in themselves, but taken together making up a series of small crises that Sylvia felt compared unfavorably in Edgar's eyes with the unruffled lives of his own relations.

And then one night Edgar's brother Arnold had called on them late, without warning, and had told them that his wife had left him three weeks earlier, declaring as she departed that she had no intention of ever coming back. She had not left him for another man. She was living on her own in a bed–sitting room in a suburb south of the river, and she had found a job in the local library.

Arnold told them all this with the detachment proper to a Manson; only the manner of his visit, unannounced and awkwardly timed, betrayed the extent of his distress. Sylvia was truly sorry for him, yet she was repelled by his stiff reserve. *When all's said and done,* she thought, *he's a dry stick.*

Yet when, after two whiskies administered by Edgar, Arnold stood up and said he must be going, Sylvia visualized the dark, empty house he would be returning to, and felt a rush of pity. "Don't go," she said impulsively. "Stay the night at least."

"Thank you, Sylvia," he replied. "That's very kind of you, but I really must go. I have things to attend to."

The milk bottle, the thermostat, the briefcase with the papers needed for the next day's work . . . Sylvia mentally shrugged her shoulders. Some people you could not help.

Edgar went to the door with his brother, and Sylvia moved about the room collecting glasses and shaking up cushions. When she heard Edgar come back in she spoke without looking around. "Poor Arnold," she said. "What a thing to happen. It's wretched for him."

"It's intolerable!" Edgar burst out, so loudly that he quite startled her. She straightened up to face him and saw that he looked quite different, his face pale, his eyes dark. She realized he was literally shaking with rage and she felt a quite pleasurable stir of excitement. "That bloody woman!" he went on. "That bitch! To walk out on him like that, after thirty-two years of marriage. For thirty-two years he's been slaving his guts out providing for her and for those children, and then when it suits her she leaves him flat!" It was as though the bitter words choked him. Bereft of speech, he pounded his right fist savagely into his left palm.

Perversely, realizing the danger, Sylvia felt impelled to defend her sister-in-law. "We don't know her side of it," she said. "She must have had her reasons."

He brushed this aside, quite literally, with his hand, as though it were a fly. "Reasons!" he said. "What reasons could she possibly have? She's got everything she could ever want or need. Just look at that house of theirs! The best of everything, a car of her own, no shortage of money. And after all, she's fifty-four, for God's sake! To run away like a damned teen-ager—I never heard of such a thing!"

"But that's what I'm getting at," she persisted. "She'd have to have a good reason for giving up so much."

"She's mad," said Edgar with flat finality, "and I've told Arnold what to do about it."

"What did you tell Arnold?"

"I told him to start divorce proceedings right away, to go and see his lawyer about it tomorrow morning, first thing."

"Divorce?" said Sylvia. "But she's only been gone three weeks! It's a bit early to be talking about divorce, surely?"

"He's well rid of her," said Edgar. "A woman who could do a thing like that, after more than thirty years! He wants to move smartly, that's what I told him, before she changes her mind and tries to come back."

"You don't think he should let her come back, then, if she wants to?"

"Let her come back? He'd be a damned fool to do anything of the sort."

"You mean you don't think Arnold should give her a second chance, after thirty-two years?"

A spasm of annoyance crossed Edgar's face. "Really, Sylvia!" he said coldly. "A second chance! You talk as though the whole thing is just a game. Once you've smashed things up you can't put them together and start again, you know."

"It's you that's talking as though it's a game!" cried Sylvia. "One slip and you're out, like being caught at cricket. In case you don't know, life's not like that. In life you just have to pick up the pieces or the ball, if you like, and keep going. Life goes on and on, after all."

"Life goes on," said Edgar, "but not necessarily marriage," and he gave her such a hostile glance that Sylvia caught her breath and realized what all this was really about.

Her first, terrified reaction was: *He knows about Terence and me,* but almost immediately she amended this to: *He suspects, or perhaps he guesses, that there is somebody.* She understood that his violent response to the defection of Arnold's wife was, perhaps unconsciously, a warning.

If he finds out definitely, if he gets any proof, he will divorce me, Sylvia said to herself, and the depth of her amazement was so profound that she knew she had never really believed this before. She had said often enough to Terence, "I'm risking my marriage. If Edgar finds out about us he will divorce me," and she had thought she meant it, but all along she must have had this deep subconscious conviction that Edgar would never do anything so extreme. Now she saw with a cold clarity that if he found out he would certainly divorce her for adultery, and that he would even fight for custody of the girls. All that, unthinkable only minutes before, was now a very real possibility.

"Margaret has certainly behaved very badly," she said hurriedly, in panic-stricken retreat, aligning herself with the securely married conventional middle-aged, but she could not tell whether Edgar even noticed her abrupt change of tone. Without acknowledging her support, he continued his diatribe against his brother's wife, and by implication all defecting wives, until well past midnight.

Long after he had fallen asleep—he lay on his back and his very breathing sounded implacably righteous to Sylvia—she lay awake, reviewing with fear and amazement the risks she had run over the previous two years. How reckless she had been, to gamble so lightheartedly with everything that she prized, and for what? For what she found she could easily in retrospect dismiss as a few evenings' pleasure. What if she and Terence had been together as many as a hundred times? What were a hundred evenings when set against a lifetime? She had been able to behave so recklessly only because she had never really believed in the risks. She had been confident first of all that Edgar would never find out, but beyond that she now discovered that she had always had an underlying comfortable feeling that even if he had found out it would not have been so dreadful. He would have been hurt and angry, she would have been penitent, there would have been painful scenes, but they would have taken place decently, in private, and afterward they would have gone on as before and nobody would ever have known about her lapse. That was what she had really believed, but now that confidence had all gone. Lying there in the dark, she knew she had been naïve. Thank God—and Arnold's wife—that she had wakened up to the danger in time. Having escaped so narrowly, she must never put herself in jeopardy again. But all this meant she must never go to the flat any more. Shaken and subdued, she vowed solemnly to herself that she would never see Terence again, except perhaps just once, in a bar or restaurant, to explain and to say good-bye. Her eyes misted over with easy tears as she imagined the parting.

Terence continued to fight against depression but only days later the inspector was back again, with the sergeant this time, and his manner was different. No more little jokes or comradely pretense. Tonight the inspector came straight to the point.

"We have reason to believe," he said, and the tone as well as the words were stiffly official, "that you were in the vicinity of Mill's Pond on the seventeenth of October last year."

Terence looked at him. "Mill's Pond?" he said. "Where the hell's that? You did say Mill's Pond, not Mill Pond?"

"Mill's Pond. You weren't there then?"

"How do I know if I was there or not when I don't know where it is? I can't possibly answer. And anyhow, who can remember anything about a night that was over a year ago? You said October, didn't you? I still had my car then. I used to do a lot of driving about; I could have passed through this Mill's Pond, I suppose."

"In point of fact, Mill's Pond is not far from here," observed the inspector. "A couple of miles or so north. The buses run from Burton."

"Oh, Mill's *Pond,*" said Terence.

"That's what I said, sir."

"But that's just a street, not a pond at all," objected Terence.

"I never said it was a pond."

"In fact, that is the street where that girl was found. . . ." Terence's voice trailed away.

"We have been approached by someone who says he saw you there. Have you any comment to make?"

"Comment? What sort of comment would you expect me to make? Who says he saw me there, anyhow?"

"*Were* you there, sir?"

"No, no, of course not. As far as I know I have never been near the place. I don't know that part at all. I never have any occasion to go over that way." He forced himself to stop. There was danger in protesting too much.

"I see," said the inspector, and left soon afterward.

Later that evening, the inspector and the sergeant were in conference at the police station.

"How do you think Lambert reacted?" the inspector asked.

"Shaken, sir, definitely shaken."

"The identification wouldn't stand up in court, though. The chap only said Lambert could have been the man he saw near Mill's Pond that night."

"He picked him out in the pub yesterday, out of a right mob of people."

"Yes, but he didn't actually say he was the man. He said he was the same type, that's all."

"Have we got enough to pull him in, then?" the sergeant asked.

"Hardly," said the inspector, "but let's recap. We've got him in the right place at the right time on two and maybe three separate occasions. We haven't got any evidence that he *wasn't* at the other places at any of the relevant times."

"No evidence that he was there, either."

"Quite so, but he hasn't been able to bring forward any evidence to prove he was anywhere else. Eight separate attacks, and no alibi for any of them."

"There *is* the long time lag, sir. In a way it would be more suspicious if he had come up with a set of cast-iron alibis."

"Fair enough, but he hasn't come up with anything at all, and the result is he could have been on the spot on all eight occasions, and he was right there on two of them by his own admission, and possibly another one, by identification. Now, what else have we got? On the attack outside the flat?"

"He was seen coming in when he hadn't said he'd been out. Miss Eves' evidence."

"Go on."

"Lambert gave a detailed description of the alleged attacker, and it was later proved in court that he couldn't have seen him at all clearly at the time."

"Right. But the anonymous note gave basically the same description."

"No evidence who wrote that, sir. Could have been Lambert himself."

"The handwriting chaps think it's unlikely Lambert wrote the address on the envelope."

"He could have got someone to do it for him," said the sergeant.

"Who could he have asked?"

"The girl friend."

"The Manson woman, you mean?"

"It could have been, sir. She's mixed up in it somehow, I swear."

The inspector looked doubtful. "Not just the friend of a key witness?" he asked.

"I suppose it's possible, sir, but somehow I don't think so. There is something that doesn't add up there."

"Let's move on. The identification? Lambert missed it at the parade, you know."

"But he got in touch immediately after the other affair. Quite definite about it, and he stuck to it."

"It rested largely on the hair."

"I wouldn't say that. He described the chap's build, clothes and way of walking."

"So he did, but there was no corroboration."

"Except the anonymous note."

"Which Lambert himself could have written. Quite so. Anything else?"

"There's Lambert's own character."

"Describe him to me."

"Divorced. Lives alone. In the habit of picking up strange women."

"By his own admission," the inspector reminded him.

"Hardly sex-starved then."

"Maybe oversexed."

"How does Mrs. Manson fit in? Would Lambert go on the prowl with a regular girl friend? She's not bad, either."

"Plenty of sex criminals with a wife and children."

The sergeant sighed. "All it seems to boil down to is that he could be the type."

The inspector agreed. "Almost anyone could be the type, outwardly," he said. "What it comes down to is that we've got a lot, but not enough."

"But it's building up, sir, isn't it?" said the sergeant. "Bit by bit."

Terence felt this himself. He felt hemmed in, threatened, and the most nightmarish thing of all was that some faceless person had apparently told the police that he had seen him at Mill's Pond on that foggy evening more than a year before. Who could he possibly be, this false witness? Was he lying or was he merely mistaken? Lying in bed that night, Terence was gripped by a choking sensation, suffocating and chilling at the same time as though he were being smothered in ice-cold feathers. The sensation was a physical one; he could not stay in bed in the dark room. He heaved himself up, threw off the covers and hit savagely at the light switch. Lit, the room looked ordinary, but not reassuring. There was something sinister in the commonplace nature of his surroundings. If this had been happening to him in a weird and exotic environment it would have been more endurable. As it was, evil had invaded his very home. He was betrayed, there was no safety anywhere. He lit a cigarette, and nerved himself to go out to the kitchen for a drink. He pulled down the blind before switching on the light but still found himself glancing nervously over his shoulder.

He filled a glass with water from the tap, impatiently, without waiting for it to run. It was lukewarm, unpleasantly metallic, but he drank it all, making the draining of the glass an act of will, an affirmation of his self-control, and then he made himself rinse the glass and dry it and put it away. As he closed the cupboard he saw himself as it were from the outside. His situation was absurd; he had to turn his back on it and start living normally. But when he went back to bed he still could not sleep.

The next day he tried to ring Sylvia. He tried several times during the day without getting her and he rang again at seven o'clock in the evening.

"Yes? Who is it?" she said, and her voice was strained with anxiety as though she were expecting bad news or an unwelcome call.

"It's me, Terence," he said.

"Why are you ringing at this time?" she said, her voice sinking to an angry whisper. "You must be mad!"

"You weren't in earlier, Sylvia. When are we going to

see each other? It's been days, almost a week."

"I can't see you," she said hurriedly. "I can't see you ever again. Can't you understand that?"

"Sylvia!"

"It's over," she hissed with panic-stricken brutality. "We're through." Then with unnatural loudness, exaggerated enunciation, "I'm sorry, you must have the wrong number," and there was a click as she hung up.

Terence was stunned, incredulous. He dialed her number again immediately and ten times more in the following hour, to be met each time by a busy signal. He had to admit to himself that she must have taken the receiver off the hook.

He rang again in the morning, sufficiently intimidated to wait until nine o'clock so that Edgar and Marion would have left, but as soon as she heard his voice she hung up without speaking, and when he rang back he found she had left the receiver off again.

He became obsessed with the need to speak to her. In his abnormal state of mind he became convinced that the two of them could work this thing out together, and only together. He went down and got a taxi to take him to the street where she lived. On arrival he directed the man to pull up a few houses away, then he found he had come out with no money and he wrote a check for an absurd amount.

Sylvia had just left the house to go to the shops when she saw Terence coming toward her. She had no wish to come on and meet him but she could not quite bring herself to run back inside and slam the door. So she stayed where she was, facing him yet poised for flight.

"I couldn't get you on the phone," he said as soon as he was within earshot, then despised himself for starting with an apology.

"You shouldn't have come here," she said. "Someone will see you—the neighbors."

"So what? You're allowed to meet a friend in the street, surely."

"You came by taxi," she pointed out. "They'd have seen you arrive."

"I didn't come right to the house," he countered. "To hell with all that anyway. We've got past the point where any of that is important."

"You may have. I haven't."

"Don't be ridiculous," he said. "For God's sake, we've got a lot more serious things to worry about than what the neighbors think."

"What things?" she said obstinately, but he ignored this and rushed on to tell her what he had decided.

"We've got to make a clean breast of everything," he declared. "Our affair, the first attack, the fact that you were the one to see it—the lot. I've been stewing over all this long enough and after all, why should I, when we can explain everything and you can give me an alibi for that night and, with any luck, for one or two of the other nights too."

"Other nights?"

"When the other girls were attacked," he said impatiently.

"You mean they suspect you of the other attacks—murders —too?"

"I told you! That's why it's got so bloody serious—but not to panic; we can fix things easily enough if we keep our heads."

"A trial costs a lot of money," she said. "I read somewhere thousands of pounds. Without your evidence they'd never even have arrested that boy, let alone brought him to trial. Naturally they're furious with you."

"He was guilty," he cried. "Guilty as hell, and you know it. Didn't you tell me he was the man you saw? Didn't you say you were absolutely sure?"

"It's all so long ago now," she said. "It's easy to make a mistake."

"That's not how you told it!"

"Sh!" she said nervously, looking around. "Let's walk on a bit, get out of this street."

He fell into step beside her. "You will do it, though, won't you?" he said urgently. "You will go to the police—ring them up, even write to them if you like. Just say you were there and saw the man, that's all."

She stopped again and looked at him. "Terence," she said, "I've told you I will never, *never* tell the police about us and that's that."

"Sylvia . . ."

"I've told you that all along," she said with a calm finality that chilled his blood. "I told you that right at the beginning and I haven't changed my mind in the least."

"But, Sylvia," he said, almost running after her as she began to walk very fast away from him. "Sylvia, there can't be any danger of its getting out now—Henderson's been acquitted. They won't—can't—try him again. And when they know about you they'll have to drop any case about me. There won't be any trial, any question of evidence being given in court."

"No," she said, "no, no, no."

He fancied a trace of rising hysteria in her voice now and she was almost running, escaping from him. He had a sudden despairing feeling that his last chance was slipping away from him.

"Wait," he said, shouting. "If you won't tell them I will! I'll go right now and tell them everything."

She turned to face him. "If you do," she said, "I'll deny it. I'll tell them you came to me this morning—as you have done —and that you tried to get me to tell lies to back you up. I'll get someone to give me an alibi for that night—Madge Stevens would do it, she'd say I was with her. She's done it once or twice before when I've been with you. And then where will you be?"

He looked at her small, smug smile and he hated her. "Bitch," he said. "Bitch, bitch, bitch."

"And anyhow, what makes the police think you are connected with those others? Maybe there are things about you I don't know. So good-bye, and don't come round here again."

She was nearly at the corner. The station was there, a train was coming. Two minutes and she would be gone forever. The gap was widening. With a leap he bridged it, grasped her shoulders, felt the cloth and the bone beneath his curving fingers.

"Sylvia!" he cried.

Her eyes blazed at him. "You're hurting me—let me go."

"Sylvia, you must help me. Can't you see? You must speak up."

"Never," she said. "How can you be so selfish?"

"Selfish? It's you who's selfish—a monster of selfishness."

"There's a train coming!" she cried, beginning to struggle. "Let me go."

He felt her straining to get away from him, he tightened his grip, moved his hands closer together, sliding them up along her shoulders toward her neck, and he saw fear come into her eyes and felt a surge of power. His breath was coming in great hissing gulps.

"Help," she screamed. "Help!" and he squeezed her throat so as not to hear her voice. Dimly he heard feet running, a whistle, hands wrenching him roughly back, so that he fell. Through a thickening mist he heard her say, "This man, he attacked me, he jumped at me from behind."

71 72 73 10 9 8 7 6 5 4 3 2